TIRED OF WAITING ON GOD

A Book on Hope, Faith, Patience and Overcoming

Life's Hurdles

Right Side Publishing

ISBN-978-1955050036

LCCN- 2021919272

This book may be purchased for educational, business or sales promotional use. For information, kindly email the author feliciacauley@ymail.com.

Published in the United States

Project manager Robert Cauley

DEDICATION

This book is for all the young people going through the

struggle of waiting

AKCNOWLEDGEMENT

I would like to thank the Lord, my savior Jesus Christ, my Husband Robert who is my number one supporter, my children, and M.O Blessing who helped bring my amazing vision to life on this book project. You are heaven sent. And to all the readers of this wonderful piece, God bless you.

TABLE OF CONTENT

INTRODUCTION

We are human and we get tired and impatient sometimes. The truth is, it takes God's grace to uphold us whenever we are overwhelmed. The same applies to Angela, a young college graduate that got sick and tired of doing everything right and still ending up with the short end of the stick. Angela who was raised by her mom Ashely and her Dad Spencer, spent most of her life with her Grandpa Miller and Grandmother Fannie Lee Peaches-Miller, where she was taught to love and obey God and his Words. Angela hung on to every teaching of her Grandma. And one can say that Grandma Peaches happens to be the biggest influence in her life, after all, she taught her mom Ashley the way of the Lord. Grandma Peaches is strong-willed while Grandpa Miller is laid back.

Ashley is somewhere in the middle; she speaks when she has to and doesn't have a problem letting everyone know Angela is her daughter. However, Ashley adores Grandma Peaches and wouldn't dare try to cross her.

Spencer on the other hand is a business man who loves his family and his job. He lets Grandma Peaches and Ashley handle things with Angela, but when he is needed, he rises to the occasion. Grandma Peaches and Grandpa Miller helped to raise Angela's cousin Tina when her parents died. Tina's father was grandma Peaches and Grandpa Miller's son. Tina has a lot of respect for her grandparents but then with a contrary opinion when it comes to religion, which often would create an argument between her and Grandma Peaches. Famous Tina; so, she thinks, believed living for Christ is not as stringent as her Grandma Peaches painted it to be. What an interesting Family!

CHAPTER ONE

IT'S GRADUATION TIME

Angela was so excited to be graduating from Spellman College; she couldn't wait to face the world waiting for her after graduation. "College is a distraction" her grandmother Mrs. Fannie Lee Peaches-Miller fondly called "Grandma Peaches" would say; "the real-life begins after college and that involves becoming financially independent which is getting a job or starting up a business and settling down to build your family." As Angela walked out of the convocation hall to locate her family members who had shown up to celebrate with her, she received some congratulatory messages from some of her friends who were already outside and taking pictures with their families. She continued to think about all the words grandma Peaches had said to her during one of the days of sitting her down to advise her, "College is just four years of the many years you have to stay on earth, but it is a very important part of your life because it will properly launch you into your future. The decisions you make here will make you or break you; the relationships you create here will probably be your biggest network."

Yes, she was excited to be graduating from college, at least one phase of her life was over, but she had uncertainties about what life had in store for her. "Hey Angela!" a familiar voice called so she paused and turned. "Karen!" she smiled. "Congratulations," they said to each other at the same time and started laughing. Karen and Angela were in the same degree program. "What are you doing tonight?" Karen asked Angela, "If there will be a party" before Angela could reply, a big tall guy crept up behind Karen unexpectedly but in a caring manner.

"Congratulation baby" Angela was puzzled at first because she had never seen the guy around the school. "Meet my boyfriend;

Joseph." Karen introduced, "he attends Dayton College. I will tell you how we met tonight." Karen whispered her last statement and smiled. In as much as Angela would love to hang out with Karen, she did not want to be a third wheel or a tag along. What was she going to be doing while the couple will be all *lovey-dovey*? "I would have love to attend Karen, but I will be having dinner with my family tonight, they travelled nineteen hours just to be here for me and besides, my roommate is leaving tomorrow, she wants me to do something for her," Angela carefully made excuses using her words. "Huh! I am not happy hearing this." Karen put on a sad face. Although those words of Angela were true, they were also excuses to avoid hanging out with the two lovers. "But do not worry, I am not leaving until Tuesday, we will catch up." She told Karen. "I have to go now, nice to meet you, Joseph." She wished them good luck and continued to locate her family, she paused halfway to turn back to see what they were doing even though she debated within herself whether to turn or not. Karen and Joseph were locking lips in the middle of the oval lawn and people were gathered around, well most of them going about their normal business; taking pictures, receiving congratulatory messages and hugging family and friends. "I thought Karen was a pastor's daughter?" she said to herself. She did not want to be judgmental but she thought Karen should have at least showed some decency in public to respect God and her father. She continued to walk to where her family members were.

Angela's grandmother had given her numerous pieces of advice about career and relationships, but she concentrated more on the former than the latter; getting a job and becoming financially independent, she told her relationships, marriage and kids will come along on its own accord. Her grandma had been a major character in her life since childhood, she had done almost everything her grandmother had told her to do and that was why she was grandma's favorite. Grandma said "don't divide your attention, don't give boys your time" and Angela stayed single through school, she had never had a boyfriend. Seeing Karen with her boyfriend earlier made her give a second thought to what her grandma had been saying to her all this while, besides, grandma wasn't innocent herself, she has had her fair share of relationships and men, she was in her third marriage. That's all Angela has heard all her life, grandma had been married three times but she dare not ask what had happened between her and the other men. "Was she stupid for listening to her grandma?" she asked herself. The school was over but there was no relationship at hand, once my family and roommate is gone, I will have to spend time alone, with no boyfriend. Maybe I will just go to the fellowship family house and hang out with my family on campus, but how can I tell some of them I don't even have boyfriends to hang out with? Well, I can testify for my friend and roommate Mary, she doesn't have a boyfriend yet, sarcastically, her name is Mary after Mary, wasn't she waiting for the right thing to do when she bears the same name with the mother of Jesus?

"God I've been waiting I've been patient I don't want to be the last one getting married and having kids among my peers,"

Angela thought to herself then began to repeat out loud "Lord don't let me be the last one you said speak those things as if they were I'm speaking it now. I don't want to be the last one Lord I've done everything that I should do, I have kept myself and refuse to sin against my own body, I have tried by your grace to keep myself faithful and pure. I do not want to be the last one to settle down; neither do I want to compromise. My faithfulness so far has to account for something." Angela huffed and puffed as she walked through the grass which was supposed to be a shortcut but it seemed so long. As she walked and talked to God, she felt herself beginning to tear up, she said to herself "oh Lord I have to get myself together the last thing I want is my family to see tears in my eyes, this is a happy day this is a happy day Lord, we will pick this up later" she said as she quickly wiped the tears off her face. As she got closer to where her family had told her they were waiting, her cousin; Tina started running towards her.

"Angela! Angela!" she called out. Angela screamed as she embraced Tina in a tight hug, they hadn't seen each other since she left home at the beginning of her final semester. Angela quickly pulled out from the hug, "Grandma Peaches is so bent on us taking pictures, don't ruin my makeup" they both laughed. "You know you look flawless with or without the makeup, always." A small smile crept onto her lips as she blushed, "Thank you." Angela raised her hand for a high five and Tina clapped hers. "Let me give you a spoiler, St. John's Baptist is organizing a welcome backslash graduation party for you when you arrive home." Tina spilled the news. "Gosh, I just can't keep it to myself. Just act surprised when grandma Peaches tell you either at dinner or when you come back. She has been announcing to everyone that her granddaughter Angela is coming back home to stay with her." Angela laughed at the revelation, she was filled with joy. The last time she saw grandma Peaches physically was at the beginning of her final semester when she went to visit her. Grandma Peaches was her maternal grandmother and she grew up in her house, she was her favorite because she has always been obedient and attentive, grandma Peaches also scored her to be emotionally intelligent. But when her father got a better job outside town, he had to relocate with Angela and his wife Ashley. Now that Angela was above eighteen and was done with college, she told her parents that she will love to go back to grandma Peaches so she could be around her, help take care of her and support her in the little way that she could. As they walked, Angela saw her family from a distance "oh my goodness!" she ran towards them, she missed them so much. Seeing them there made her feel like she hadn't seen them in forever especially her grandmother. She and her grandma were always on a video call, talking, discussing, and planning her graduation party. Angela loves her grandmother so much that she always mentions her. Some of the friends she met in college thought that her mother had passed away and that she was raised by her grandmother but she always corrected them when they brought it up. Her mom was her mom and her grandmother was her grandmother, they both have their own role in her life.

Angela ran into her grandma's open arms "my baby!" she cried, I am so proud of you." She rained kisses on her cheeks. Standing next to grandma Peaches was her mother Ashley, who also joined in on the hug, when everyone saw that they were getting emotional, they began to join in on the hug, and it became a big family group hug. Angela was the first in her family to graduate from Spellman College and it made them even more proud of her. Grandma Peaches had come with a professional photographer; her cousin Bastille. She said she did not want that backyard back in the day pictures young people take with their cell phones; she wanted it to be standard and organized. Grandma Peaches asked everyone to gather and arrange themselves, "This is once in a lifetime, we have to make it look right so listen to the photographer and do what he says." She wanted to make everything perfect for Angela because those were the pictures she will use to look back on this day and bring nostalgia. They took lots of photos, grandma Peaches said she will sit with Bastille later to select the finest ones that he will print. After the pictures, they decided to go to their hotel on prepare for dinner in an exquisite restaurant while Angela will go back to her dorm, drop her gown, and then prepare for dinner too. Angela planned on bringing her friend Mary to dinner with her family because Mary's family couldn't make it, they promised to celebrate her when she gets back home and her flight was scheduled for the next day afternoon. She knew Mary had nowhere else to go after the convocation ceremony because she was always by herself and not sociable. She was a leader in their campus fellowship and always tried her best to lead by example; she was always so self-conscious about everything and anything and mostly kept to herself. She was so keen on keeping herself from temptation and that had helped her through school. She may have been a Christian sister but she was smart enough to know when a guy was fooling around and she was bold enough to tell her friends that "he isn't the one" or "he is not attracted to you." They all walked to the parking lot meant for visitors, and Angela told them that she will see them later. "Don't keep us waiting." Grandma Peaches told her before she got into the car. Then she decided to walk to the other side of the parking lot. Students and grandaunts had parked their cars. Angela wanted to walk alone and reflect on her conversation with her creator before she met with her family. "Lord, I think I am ready for a relationship, I am tired of waiting for him to come to me. Maybe it is my fault for not wanting to be in a relationship while in school. But Lord Jesus, I'm ready now." Just then, she hears a faint voice say to her, "he who findeth a wife findeth a good thing." She quiets herself and says, "I hear you, Lord, you got my back and that's enough assurance. I'm good!" She was still communing with God when a voice broke her from her thoughts. "Angela!" a thick voice called. It was a male, who could that be? She thought to herself. She turned back slowly to see who he was, "Charles!" she called smiling. "Yes baby, it's me." He walked closer. Charles was her childhood friend from the same neighborhood; he attended Morehouse College which was just a few kilometers from Spellman. "What are you doing here at Spellman?" she asked him. "I came to see you congratulate you in person." He said to her. Angela and Charles continued to communicate on social media even after she left town. Charles brought his friend with him. "Meet my roommate James" he introduced the guy to her and they shook hands. "Nice to finally meet you Angela" he smiled, "nice to meet you too" Angela replied. "My graduation is in three days," Charles announced to Angela.

"Congratulations Charles, but I won't be able to attend; I have booked my flight for Tuesday already." Charles shrugged, "No problem, we can always communicate when we get back home, let me give you my number, you know I got mad love for you, I wish I would have done things differently in the past, then in the future, we would be like some of those couples who knew each other from high school, went to colleges not far from each other and got married" he chuckled. Angela just smiled, Charles had always teased her about liking her but she didn't quite understand what he meant by if he had done things differently, "but who knows, anything can happen, I am not going to push too hard by asking for your number, when you get back home and you need a friend, know that I am always here and we could hang out." He called out his digits as she typed them on her phone, "saved. I will call." She told him. "How is Grandma Peaches?" Charles asked. Everyone who knew Angela knew grandma Peaches because she talked about her grandma a lot and when she was home, they were always seen together, doing groceries shopping, accompanying grandma Peaches to her hospital appointments and even going to church together. "She was around a while ago, I will be meeting up with them for dinner" she responded. "Grandma Peaches" Charles smiled, "always so protective of you then, she didn't let you do anything or go anywhere out of her sight, it is a miracle she let you attend college far away from home." He gave a sardonic laugh.

"Charles, I'm no longer a child, I am a college graduate. Don't insult me." "No! it's not that, It is more of a compliment about how well you were able to cope on your own without being under your grandma's radar." Only if he knew how many times they talked in a week she smiled under her breath. "Do you have a boyfriend Angela?" Charles asked.

Why is he asking me such a question? Angela thought in her head. "Yes I do, he has graduated, and he is working now." She lied.

She knew she wanted a man but was Charles the right candidate? Charles wasn't exactly a church boy like her, in high school, he was known as the bad boy who had women at the snap of his fingers, it was a good thing he was able to make it to college and graduate. But what if he's changed she asked herself. I mean, he was able to focus in school and lead a good life and why did he appear when she was having a conversation with God about a man. She pulled out from her thoughts and continued the conversation with Charles and his friend, they talked about their majors, plans after graduation and how one of her cousins was going to help her take her car home while she took a plane. She checked her time and it was past four, she informed Charles and his friend James that she had to go so she could squeeze out time to rest before it is time to meet up with her family members.

She hugged Charles and softy whisper into his ears, "goodbye." She could feel him sniff her hair. Was it a good sign? She was never really close to guys so she couldn't tell. She made a mental note to discuss it with her cousin Tina because she was more exposed than her when it came to issues like this. "You are a strong woman Angela, your parents and your grandma did a good job in raising you, hold on to your faith no matter what, I have been in college for the past four years and the girls I have encountered made my respect for you to increase. I understand that women are not to be blamed completely for their wrongs, I mean men have a hand in it too but women are the gatekeepers, they ought to set standards for their selves and if a man loves them enough, he will respect their wish and stand by them. All I am saying is I appreciate the way you were raised, but I appreciate you more for holding on because not everyone who was given such training continued to hold on to it when they left home." Angela smiled. She looked at Charles and wondered how fast he had matured.

"Thank you so much, for everything; for coming, for the compliment, I appreciate it." Angela turned and continued walking to her car. Charles and James just stood there, watching her every move, as her foot touches the end of the grass, as she stepped down from the curve, even when her figure became very visible, he admired her even more. "God, you have made wonderful species," he said to himself as she got out of sight.

CHAPTER TWO

THE BEGINNING OF THE END

When Angela got to her dorm room, she met her roommate taking a nap which made her tiptoed further into the room so as not to make any disturbing sound. She puts down her graduation gown and other accessories. She was so exhausted from the entire activities of the day; from the convocation ceremony itself to the greeting and congratulatory wishes, lots and lots of pictures taken and even her little conversation with her God. She decided to take a nap before she and Mary goes out for dinner with her family. With a sigh of relief, she slouched on her bed and fell off to sleep almost immediately.

It was almost time for dinner when Angela woke up from her nap, she had slept for almost 2 hours and it felt like thirty minutes, she struggled to stand up from her bed because she was still very sleepy. Her Grandma's call awakened her more; "Hello Grandma" she answered sleepily. "Goodness gracious, are you sleeping child?" she asked surprised. "No! I'm awake." She answered quickly before grandma Peaches could say more. "Was that a lie?" she thought to herself, but it wasn't, she wasn't lying. She wasn't asleep but not in the way her grandma knew. "Alright child, I just wanted to let you know that we are about to leave for the restaurant, meet us there, you should leave your dorm as soon as possible."

"Do not worry grandma, I will be there as soon as possible" as soon as I finish dressing up she said with her inner voice. She quickly stood up to her dresser and began to search for a gown suitable for her outing, she thought of wearing her graduation gown to the restaurant but her inner pretty being protested against it. She picked up a beautiful nude-colored gown and matched it with a black beautiful sandal. She walked over to

Mary's bed before she went into the bathroom to have her bath. When they were done dressing up, they both walked down to the car park and drove to the restaurant. It was a Japanese steakhouse, her family members were already inside, waiting for her to arrive. "Hope I didn't keep you all waiting for long?" she asked as she and Mary got to their table. She walked over to grandma Peaches and kissed her on her cheeks, then placed another kiss on her mother's cheek; she was seated next to grandma Peaches. "No dear, we arrived here not long ago." Angela's cousin.

Zack brought out a chair and offered Mary to sit down, she had been standing while Angela went round to greet everyone. When she was done with exchanging pleasantries, she was asked to seat at the head of the table because she was the celebrant of the day. "What do you think about the restaurant? Angela's dad asked her, "it's exquisite, I like it or what do you think Mary?" she asked her roommate. "I do like this place." She smiled. Even though their school was close by, they didn't come here because it was an exquisite restaurant and it was quite expensive for students. The waiter came to take their order. When their steak arrived, everyone ate and talked about their family's happy moments and Angela's childhood and also informed her about the graduation party St. John's Baptist Church was organized for her, Angela shouted a fake "Yay!" just so grandma Peaches will not suspect that her dearest cousin Tina had broken the news to her already. When they were done with the main course, grandma Peaches ordered desserts for everyone, "I'm celebrating my baby girl." She said happily, "she has graduated."

After dinner, they took some more pictures and Angela hugged her family and they said their goodbyes to each other, "I will see you all before you leave tomorrow" she told them as she and her roommate saw them off to their cars. "Let me know when you get back to your dorm" grandma Peaches told Angela. "Yes ma'am" she called as she walked over to her car.

Soon as she got back into her dorm, she remembered she had met Charles during the day. He had grown, he was like a little brother to her then, he was older than her by a few months, yeah, but he use to have a small stature. Angela use to defend him and act like a big sister to him until she left during her sophomore year when her father got transferred out town. In a few years, Charles had grown, he was looking so handsome when she saw him earlier, she had never romantically thought about Charles until earlier when he popped out of nowhere in the middle of her conversation about a relationship and family with God. He even asked her if she had a boyfriend and complimented her about her character. He had given her his number, was she going to call him when she got back? She didn't want to seem desperate but then, they used to be friends and there was no harm in calling to hang out with him, it wasn't like she had a job yet or had other engagements. "I would like to see him again." She whispered.

******

At Charles's house, there was a mini party. Their guests were drinking and smoking with loud music playing. Charles wasn't always an insanely Christian boy, yes, he went to church back in the day but he wasn't exactly devoted. He had women in his corner, took alcohol and didn't attend weekly activities. "You! Charles, tell us about your little girlfriend you went to see at Spellman today." Tom, Charles's friend tapped him on his shoulder. His friends had overheard him talking with James about going to see Angela at her school. "James said you were smitten." Tom teased. Charles had always been smitten by Angela, he had always admired how she carried herself with dignity as a strong Christian woman and even after coming to college, and she never lost her virtues. Anyone who was close friends with Charles would have heard him talk about her either passively or actively and that was why James insisted on going to her graduation with Charles. "She is not my girlfriend yet and she is a different girl I respect a lot. I will not sit here and let you talk about her in some disrespectful manner." Charles cautioned.

"You like this one" Tom laughed.

"As I said, she is different" Charles reiterated. "I mean, she is so pure, I know she told me she had a boyfriend earlier but I knew she was lying," Charles had always known Angela to be a bad liar and he didn't miss the slight stutter when she said yes, she had a boyfriend. Besides, he knew Angela will never do anything outside of what grandma Peaches tells her to do. That girl had never been in a relationship, she is a freaking virgin. Angela needs a man, she needs a man, and she has been by herself for far too long. "Is she aware of what you do? Does she know that you have a son?" Tom asked. "With the way you have described her, she will never have anything to do with you if she knows the real you." "You have a son?" James asked Charles as he walked in on their discussion. He had a red plastic cup half-filled with alcohol in his hand. "How come I didn't know about this?"

"Because it is not something I am proud of." Charles placed his hand on his head and rubbed his face.

"Something that you are not proud of but will eventually hunt your relationship if you decide to start anything with her." Tom cautioned.

"It is even worse than you guys think. I just don't have a son; I am married to my son's mother." Charles said in a harsh whisper. James spewed his drinks from his mouth. "This is a lot to take in, I can't believe that we have been friends for years and I don't even know these things about you man." James' eyes opened.

"It is because I am not proud of it, she was my high school girlfriend. It was supposed to be just a fling but she got pregnant, I didn't even like her that much." "I am confused myself, man. I knew you have a child but you never mentioned anything about marriage."

"I come from a small town, they are religious people.

Stephanie was a church girl, when she got pregnant, her parents were furious. They were strongly against premarital sex and had us wedded by a priest before she gave birth to cover the shame they will face as elders in the church."

"Why did you agree to it? People get pregnant all the time, it is either they opt for an abortion or they become single parents, forcing the both of you to get married because of an unwanted pregnancy is so out of it, what did your father say?"

"He didn't want to have a hand in it; he said if I was responsible I should handle it, he said he will support me in the little way he can while I am here in college but I will have to be financially responsible for them."

"I have to use the restroom." Charles lied. The whole conversation had weighed him down and he just wanted to be alone with his thoughts. He walked away from his two friends and made his way to his room. He opened the door and found two people kissing and groping on his bed. "Yuck!" he closed the door immediately. One of the insane things about hosting a party, He couldn't even be angry because he had also done the same when he attended parties at another's house. Either it was just a one-night stand or the girl he was with at that moment. When Charles left for college, he never for once took his wedding vows seriously. He liked Stephanie enough to sleep with her but not enough to be his wife. Heck! He wasn't even ready for marriage when he was forced to take those vows at the altar with just Stephanie's parents, her younger sister and his father in attendance. He walked out of the house and into the street. Life had been a mess for him. He was just a young boy who wanted to have fun and live life in the little way he could. He remembered the day he found out that Stephanie was pregnant. She had tricked him into escorting her to see the doctor.

She was an asthmatic patient and she told him it was one of her appointments. When they got to the clinic, they both sat down in the waiting room and she seemed anxious. "Why are you anxious?"

he asked her. Was she supposed to be? When it was time for her consultation, she insisted he went in with her.

"Am I supposed to go in there? It's your appointment, I will wait here." He didn't like hospitals, especially consultation rooms. He remembered that was where a doctor had broken the news to him and his dad that he had lost his mother to the cold hands of death when he was just twelve years old. He could still perceive the smell of drugs and antiseptic that lingered in the air, how neatly the doctor's office was arranged. He was wearing a scrub and a cap to cover his hair. He had just finished operating on her. He didn't know he was going to accompany Stephanie into the doctor's office. She had tricked him to come there; she knew exactly how he felt about hospitals. "Sit down" the doctor ordered them when they entered his consultation room. They both sat down. "How are you doing?" he asked Stephanie. "You seem to have improved."

"Yes, doctor" she nods her head as she replied to the doctor. "Your test results are here." He told her as he went through a series of envelopes that were carefully arranged on his table.

"Here you go," he says as he handed the white envelope to her.

"Huh, what it says?" she asks him nervously.

"The result is in your hand, Stephanie." He raised a brow.

"I'm nervous, it will be better if you just tell me."

"Well Stephanie, the last time you came here, you complained about some symptoms that you have been feeling, so I asked them to take your urine and blood samples, the results came in, you are pregnant." He blurted. Charles remembered how he felt blood drained from his face when he heard what the doctor said. Is this true? If Stephanie is pregnant then was he the father? That fateful day was the beginning of so many wrongs that happened in his life. He didn't want Stephanie to know how freaked out he was so he asked her to go home while they talk about it the next day. Angela called him that night because her mother found the test result lying on her bed and had demanded to see who was responsible for her pregnancy.

He wasn't proud of what had happened but he took responsibility for his actions. Charles quickly informed his dad

what had happened and pleaded he accompany him to Stephanie's house. When they arrived at Stephanie's house,

Stephanie and Charles became the subject of discussion, Stephanie's parents scolded them and stated how disappointed they were for being so careless with their selves. They said two sins cannot make things right and they can never support abortion, Stephanie will have to give birth to the baby and Charles will be there for her, they both had to find a way to make things work. Charles's father Nathan told them that his son had gotten accepted into college and he will not forfeit his education for anything. They accepted as long as he agreed to get married before going and found a way to care for his wife and the baby's needs. Stephanie was angry because she had to be the one to face most of the consequences, she had to stop school and nurse her baby. But Charles still had a choice; little did she know that it was harder on his path because getting money wasn't so easy. Despite knowing that he was a college student who got his fees from his father, she still called for baby food, diapers and her upkeep initially until the baby became three years old. She had to find a job at a café to support their needs and lift the weight from Charles but even at that, he still provided the majority of their needs. Before he left for College, desperation for money made him associate with some bad gang members and he started to sell drugs. He hoped that after college, he will get a good job and quit the dirty job he was doing, he was an intelligent student and he knew it would not take him long. Stephanie and his baby were currently staying in her parents' house and he will have to get an apartment when he gets back. His feeling for Stephanie wasn't so intense for him to spend the rest of his life with her, he was ready to be there for his baby but she wasn't in his plan. The only woman he truly had eyes for was Angela, but because of how protective her grandma was of her back then, it made it difficult for him to let her know about his feelings. When her father got transferred they had to temporarily move out of town.

"Ahhhhhhhh, jeez!" Charles lets out a groan. He felt frustrated. For years, he had kept this secret to himself and now he had to face everything in just a few days.

CHAPTER THREE

WELCOME BACK PARTY

The following week, Angela went back home, her family were so excited to see her like they didn't just depart a few days ago. Her cousin Zack helped her carried her bag into her room while grandma Peaches treated her to a nice welcome back meal. After lunch, she decided to take a nap to relieve herself from the stress of travelling. She got into her room and realized that her room was exactly the way it had always been, she was surprised that grandma Peaches had left the room unaltered; her family portrait was still sitting on her chest drawer beside her bed, her paintings and note tags were still stuck to her wardrobe. The only thing that had changed was her bedspread, she was sure grandma Peaches had just changed it before she arrived. She lay down carefully on the bed and caressed her pillows until she fell asleep.

On Friday, the family began the preparations for the graduation slash welcome back party in honor of Angela. Everyone was busy; grandma Peaches and Ashley were doing the meal preparation; marinating chickens and slicing vegetables, while Tina was making the dough for the pastries. Angela was rehearsing her graduation speech; she practiced several times in front of two audiences, namely her grandma Peaches and her cousin.

"Am I doing it right?" she asked.

"Yeah," Tina replied.

Michelle Angela's childhood friend and best friend who was also a member of St. John's Baptist Church came around to help out in the preparation for the big night, she helped to arrange fresh flowers in the glass jars in the garage. She loved to decorate and that was her motivation to join the decoration group in church; they decorated the altar in church and occasionally would decorate the entire church during special occasions. Before Michelle got married she would always spend time in Grandma Peaches house on the first week of every December just for Christmas decorations. Putting the piece of paper away, Angela asked her grandma, "Can I help in making the lemonade?"

"No" grandma Peaches responded to her.

"Please" Angela pleaded, trying to mimic puppy eyes just so grandma Peaches will get carried away.
"Tomorrow is your big day," Grandma Peaches told her,

"I can't stress you out."

"I know," she affirmed.

"You need to sleep early tonight." Grandma Peaches told her.

"Okay, good night," Angela said and headed to her bedroom.

She set her alarm at 5:00 a.m. for prayer as her bedtime ritual and jumped into bed. She patted her shoulder for accomplishment, she was happy she could make her parents and grandmother proud of her. Before she drifted off to sleep, she wished she had a man to share her joys and thoughts with, he would have attended this party that was being hosted for her and would be super proud. They will hold hand in hand appreciating guests for coming and he will be like a member of their family just like the way grandma Peaches brought her dad closer to herself. "I am going to keep holding on and believing that my church boy will come my way." She said to herself and smiled. She had always imagined her future husband to be a person who grew up in the church, obeyed constituted authorities, was family-oriented and was a faithful lover. She had read many books especially Christian novels which made her faith stronger and made her firm in her belief that love is the most beautiful feeling and people who loved and are loved back in relationships are the happiest people on earth. "Another night of sleeping single" She smiled to herself, turned off the lights by her bedside and drifted off to sleep.

The next afternoon, Angela started to go get ready for the graduation party, her cousin Tina was in her room to help her with her makeover. "You have done a good job."

Grandma Peaches complimented Tina as she traced the nude lip gloss on Angela's pouty lips. "Thanks, grandma Peaches."

Tina smiled; she barely got compliments from grandma Peaches. "Smack your lips together." She told Angela who was sitting down in front of Tina's ring light looking pretty.

"You look beautiful Angela." Grandpa Peaches complimented Angela.

"Thanks, grandma." She responded to the compliment. Grandma Peaches leaned and gave Angela a hug, Tina who was standing next to them playfully rolled her eyes.

"Yes, I know she is your favorite granddaughter and you

cannot get enough of her but can you please let me finish the makeup?" Tina requested.

"I do not have a favorite grandchild, I love you both."

Grandma Peaches told Tina as she unwrapped herself from Angela's embrace. Even though grandma Peaches had never agreed to the fact that Angela was her favorite granddaughter, everyone knew, her actions spoke louder than words. The grandmother and daughter have had a tremendous unbreakable bond since Angela was a newborn. People have mistaken Angela for her biological daughter because they look alike; light-skinned, small frame body, perfect set of white teeth and thick natural hair. "I am just so proud of everything she has achieved. You made it honey." As she was walking out of the room, she paused by the door and began dancing. If only she could twerk.

"Go grandma, go grandma…" Tina started cheering her.

"Go grandma, go, grandma…" Angela continued.

"Get it; get It!" her granddaughters were singing as she moved her body.

"Shake, grandma, shake it!" She stopped dancing and told Angela her favorite verse about education.

"The fear of the Lord is the beginning of knowledge; fools despise wisdom and instructions Proverbs 1:7." Her cousin rolled her eyes again as if she were 'allergic' to Bible verses.

"You two get ready. I am going to set the table." Grandma Peaches said and finally exited the bedroom. She opened the kitchen door and headed to the backyard. It was decorated in blue, yellow, and white colors. Twenty round tables with five chairs in each, Ivory roses on each table and balloons arranged well. There were red rose petals on the ever-green lawn.

"Michelle did a good job." Grandma Peaches said to herself. While the girls were alone in the bedroom, Tina started a conversation with Angela.

"I still do not get why grandma Peaches refused to hire a DJ for this party, I mean why do we have to listen to gospel music today?" Tina asked Angela. "I can get you a local artist to perform," she said. Her cousin was a social media influencer, but she acted like a big celebrity in the neighborhood.

Angela remained quiet for a second pondering her thoughts. Gospel music is the only music she knows. "I only listen to songs which glorify our God," she said.

"Girl bye!" Tina blurted out. "You don't know what you are missing," she said. "Not all secular songs glorify Satan, songs are pure love songs, songs about life and the rest. This is your big day dear cousin, you have to vibe to the fullest." "I know it is my big day, but I cannot seem to forget God on one of the biggest days of my life," Angela believed in God completely "Besides, most of the people attending are our church members even Pastor Brown will be there."

"You are indeed grandma Peaches favorite daughter because you act like her." Tina shook her head, she felt like Angela was too focused on what she was told to do or act like than experiencing life for herself and living her life. She had always lived for grandma Peaches. "I don't have a problem with that," Angela replied with a half-smile showing off her white pearly teeth. She would rather act like Grandma Peaches than Tina.

The former is wiser and she never had any ugly encounters since she has been guided by grandma Peaches, she believed grandma Peaches have had so many encounters and lessons from life and will do a good job leading her in the right direction. Angela and Tina did not have the same perspective about life, although, Tina loves God she doesn't go overboard to show it. She is independent in her decisions, she doesn't need grandma Peaches to direct her every step but believes that her relationship with God will lead her down the right path. Grandma Peaches kept saying that she was very stubborn and unyielding and sometimes she could not stand her.

Tina did not grow up with grandma Peaches, so she did not see a reason to act just like her. She understood that she could still be herself, mingle with boys, listen to a different kind of music and still have a relationship with God. What matters the most was herself preservation, Tina was not trying to please anyone.

After a silent moment between the two ladies, Angela smiled and handed her stud earrings to Tina to help her put on her ears. "Done" Angela stood up and admired her face in the mirror. "Let's go out tonight, after the party." Tina offered. She did not notice that Grandma Peaches was back and standing behind her at the door.

"Tina!" she called out loud.

"Angela will go for no such thing, what is she going to enjoy in that other party that she will not enjoy here in the presence of her family, both biological and in faith?" Tina rolled her eyes before turning to face grandma Peaches. "Grandma Peaches, I think Angela is old enough to know what is right or wrong for her, I am not forcing the suggestion down her throat, she has a right to decline if she wishes to."

"Be careful." She warned. "She is a good girl and an unashamed church girl…"

"…Unlike me who worships the devil." Tina cuts grandma Peaches off. They were always on each other's tail when it

came to issues like this. Grandma Peaches will always look for a way to condemn her lifestyle at every given opportunity but never saw any wrong in whatever Angela did because she was her puppet.

"Oh you two, please stop!" Angela shouted, she had to put an end to their bickering for the night because those two could go on and on for the whole night until one person gets tired or frustrated and decided to retire to their room. "At least, not today." She warned them. "Your guests are waiting, let us go to the backyard. Pastor

Brown is here, everyone cannot wait to see you." Grandma Peaches told Angela.

As they were all walking out of the room, Tina tickled grandma Peaches. "Stop it you naughty child, you have no respect for your grandmother." She laughed.

"I love you grandma Peaches, you are the best in the world." Tina teased as they all walked out of the room. Grandma Peaches and Tina might not always be on the same page, but they loved each other dearly.

Angela was wearing a royal blue skirt suit with a matching hat, a nice pewter pearls bead around her neck, she preferred pearl to gold and silver because her skin reacts with metal necklaces or earrings. "Is this a Sunday service or a party?" Tina asked on the way to the backyard. "Darn!" she continued to complain. "Praise the Lord," the reverend said, and then he commenced the graduation and welcome back party with an opening prayer. The choir sang worship songs for a few minutes, Angela knelt to reverence God and thanked him for keeping her alive and bringing her thus far. Afterwards, they sang her most favorite hymn, she was given the honor to lead the hymn. She used to be an active member of the choir before she left town.

In Christ alone my hope is found;

He is my light, my strength my song;

This cornerstone, this solid ground,

Firm through the fiercest drought and storm;

What heights of love, what depth of peace, When fear is stilled, when strivings cease!

My comforter, my all in all – Here in the love of Christ, I stand.

In Christ alone, who took on flesh?

The fullness of God in helpless babe

This gift of love and righteousness

Scorned by the one he came to save

'Til on that cross, as Jesus died

The wrath of God was satisfied

For every sin, on him, was laid

Here, in the death of Christ, I live

There in the ground, his body lay

Light of the world, by darkness, slain

Then bursting forth in glorious day

Up from the grave, he rose again

And as he stands in victory

Sin's curse has lost its grip on me

For I am his and he is mine

Bought with the precious blood of Christ

No guilt in life, no fear in death

This is the power of Christ in me

From life's first cry to final breath

Jesus commands my destiny

No power of hell, no scheme of man

Can ever pluck me from his hand

'Til he returns or calls me home

Here, in the power of Christ, I stand

No power of hell, no scheme of man

Can ever pluck me from his hand

'Til he returns or calls me home

Here, in the power of Christ, I stand.

What heights of love, what depth of peace, When fear is
stilled, when strivings cease!

My comforter, my all in all – Here in the love of Christ, I stand.

By the time Angela was done leading the hymn, trickles of tears flowed down her cheeks, the song always resonated with her spirit. Her emotion rubbed off on most of the people who attended the ceremony. Afterwards, the anchor of the event came up and introduced the dignitaries present; the senior pastor of St. John's Baptist Church, Pastor Brown, his beautiful wife; Julie and kids; Isaiah and Isabelle, the associate pastor and his family, the elders present, the women leader, men leader and the youth leader, even grandma Peaches was introduced as a dignitary. Angela was asked to come on stage for her speech. After the speech, a young girl climbed the stage carrying a neatly folded sash and the youth pastor was called forth to decorate her with it. Everyone clapped. The meals began to go round and everyone ate to their satisfaction. And when the party was over, St. John's Baptist church gave Angela a check as a graduation gift. "Thank you everyone for honoring me, I pray that

God will take you to a point where people will celebrate you. God bless you richly." Angela appreciated them. "Nice party, but I could not get anything to drink." Tina walked up behind Angela where she was sitting with her mom and Michelle. "Are you serious?" Angela was surprised. "But we stocked the house with enough that will be ready to go round."

"I know, there are drinks everywhere, but I could not get anything to drink. No alcohol." She stated. Angela rolled her eyes. "There wasn't even anything as simple as red wine, there isn't anything wrong with it." Tina sulked. "When hosting parties in this house, the organizers," she said emphasize the last word and directing her gaze to Ashley who was seated with Angela on the table "Should please consider everyone's preferences." Ashley smiled and stood up from the table leaving the two cousins to their selves, she was tired and did not have any strength left in her to engage her niece; Tina. "This feels like I attended the graduation ceremony of a child just done with kindergarten, you should have brought a trampoline knew her cousin too well to get unnecessarily offended by some of her words. Despite their differences in lifestyle, the cousins love each other, occasionally; guests would come to greet Angela before going. Tina's eyes travelled around the crowd, she had a comment or two about most of them, Michelle and Angela would just laugh it off, Tina was full of humor. When her eyes got to the pastor's table, she spotted his son, sitting next to his younger sister, they were talking to each other. "I admire him," Tina said. It drew the attention of Angela and Michelle.

"Who?" Michelle asked.

"The Pastor's son, of course, I respect him so much, he knows the effect he has on the young ladies in our church but has never for once misused it. You know I hear everything, I have not heard a negative or derogatory rumor about him yet." She told them. "Effect on young women?" Michelle asked. "Just look" she used her eyes to direct them to two girls sitting at a table adjacent to where the Pastor's kids were sitting, they were looking at him and were gushing over him.

"That isn't the first I have noticed tonight and even on Sundays." She told them.

"Wow, you are quite observant," Michelle stated. "What do I care, I go back home the same way I carry myself to church. Now that Angela is back, she might be the reason I will stay back after services to chat, if not when there are no women meetings or service unit meetings, what else do I have to do than go back to my husband's house."

"That's how she does, instead of her focusing on what the pastor is saying, she is always busy focusing on who is crushing on the Pastor's son."

"It is not rocket science and I am not the only one who has noticed it, especially when he is seated at the piano stand."

"Are you sure you are not crushing too?" Angela asked her cousin, she was too invested in this issue.

"No!" Tina shouted. Michelle busted out laughing.

"I agree that I crushed on him at a point but it didn't go beyond that, besides he is not my kind of man so the crush did not last." "Are you sure?" Michelle asked teasingly.

"Yeah" she replied. "Thinking about it, I could just catch fun." She bit her lower lips.

"I'm going to talk to him; I will ask for his number." She prepared to stand. "Tina, let it go," Angela warned she knew

her cousin; she was audacious and will do just as she has said. "What do you need his number for?"

"I need prayers, can't I ask a pastor's son to pray for me?" she said flirtatiously. Everyone knew Isaiah was a man of God and was never caught flirting or in a compromising position with any woman in church no matter the circumstance.

"Go to the source, ask his dad for prayers instead" Michelle replied.

"The source is God and not Pastor Brown." Angela thought Tina was just being Tina, she didn't know that she was serious about going to him.

"Ok, fine. I will still talk to him, but not right now." She smiled. Angela thought about Tina's boldness, she is so courageous, bold and she was quite sure of whom she was, it was quite easy for her to strike conversations with everyone including the opposite sex. Angela who had never dated anyone in her life talk less of having a serious boyfriend kept on consoling herself with grandma Peaches words that if she waited for the right time, she will be a wife and a mother to a God-sent husband and God-fearing children. Despite her significant achievement in life, one thing was needed to fix the jigsaw puzzle-a future husband. That piece was still missing in a puzzle. Sometimes she could wake up in the middle of the night and wonder.

Where is Mr. Right? She would think and sigh.

At 9:00 p.m. graduation ceremony was supposed to end according to the program. Instead, the pastor stood up and prayed again. "Amen," the guests said as he finished praying. "Please come to church on time tomorrow, "he told his congregation, who were at a graduation party."

"Don't forget to bring offerings too." Pastor Brown teased, and people laughed. Then he reminded his church members to go to sleep early as the next day was Sunday. Grandma Peaches thanked everyone for coming to her granddaughter's party out of their busy schedule on behalf of the family.

Michelle's husband who had missed the party because of work came to pick his wife up. "You should go to bed now." Grandma Peaches walked up to Angela and said to her. "I need my beauty sleep too." She added.

Grandma Peaches walked inside the house, some of the guests

were still outside in the backyard, talking to each other. Angela felt tired and sleepy, she didn't do much to prepare for the party but during the event, she smiled till her cheeks hurt.

She rubbed her eyes and grabbed a cupcake and went inside. Angela went into her bedroom and slammed the door; she could still hear the gospel music coming from the speakers, she looked through the window and saw Tina standing next to Isaiah, they were having a conversation. She finds it difficult to do what Tina did, she was not very approachable by men with the way she carries herself and she didn't know how to get men's attention but Tina who just made a joke about it was already standing next to him. She shifted her gaze to the other side and saw Sister Rita talking to one of the church elders. She walked away from the window and stood in front of her vanity mirror; she glanced at herself for ten minutes. She asked herself why she wasn't approachable. "Even Tina and Sister can draw the attention of the opposite sex but I can't, I do not even have one to call my own." It's still a big puzzle that Latoya has an offender ankle bracelet, not ashamed of it. She wore a romper showing off her legs and bracelet. She did not care for people to judge her. Sister Rita had no teeth. Still, men flirted with her all the time in the Bible study. Angela denied it in her heart but she felt slightly jealous of Tina on that day, not because she spoke to Isaiah but because she possessed the kind of strength and boldness that she admired. She was never scared to go for what she wanted and was always ready to take full responsibility if they did not turn out well. She took off her clothes and changed into her nightwear, she went back to the window to spy and saw Isaiah shook hands with Tina with a broad smile plastered on his face, they even exchanged phone numbers, she quickly checked up on Sister Rita who was enjoying a bowl of soup while she continued her conversation with the church elder. Isabelle who looked extra bored walked up to her parents who were by a flower pot taking pictures, Pastor Brown took one small part of the flower and positioned it on Julie's hair, she looked thrilled and placed a feathery kiss on her husband's lips.

The three of them walked to where Isaiah was standing with Tina they got into a conversation, Angela closed the curtain and knelt beside her bed to say her night prayers, not forgetting to chip in the part where she wanted God to speed up the process of her meeting her right man. She finished her prayers and jumped into bed and fell asleep almost immediately.

CHAPTER FOUR

A NEW JOB

The next day was Sunday; she woke up by 6am and took a shower, she had forgotten to prepare what she will wear to church on that fateful Sunday and was opting for wearing an oversized maxi dress and flat shoes, they were the easiest to access at that moment. Tina walked into her room and sat on her bed.

"You are not going to church today?" Angela asked her.

"Nope." She answered.

"Why?" Angela asked. She did not know what was her cousin's reason for not going to church, she will not be allowed to use the excuse of she is tired because she was not the only one who prepared for the previous night party

"Because I do not feel like it!" She replied seeming uninterested with the series of questions Angela was asking.

"You do not serve God only when it is convenient for you Tina…"

"…And who says I won't say my prayers here in the house, who said I will not even sing songs of worship. I just do not feel like going to church, that's all." She shrugged.

"Do not forsake the assembling of ourselves together, as the manner of some is; but exhorting one another: and so much the more, as ye see the day approaching Hebrews 10:25." Angela quoted for Tina but she seemed even more uninterested.

"Here, Isaiah wanted me to give you this, he really wanted to hand it to you himself but you did not even come downstairs again till all the guests left.

You left me alone to bid them all farewell before going inside." She handed the gift to Angela.

"Thanks." She took the gift from Tina and kept it on her bedside table. "I saw you guys talking yesterday." She commented. "Yeah, I walked up to him to strike a conversation; we were talking about the last basketball game." She replied, "But you don't like sports," Angela told her. Tina knew her game and played well too. She watched the news and sports channel, only to catch up with the conversation when talking to a man. She knew for sure men either love to talk about politics or sports, period.

"I thought Isaiah is shy," Angela said.

"He is hilarious," Tina told her. Angela and Isaiah were not really friends, they were just church members, "What else were you talking about?" She was curious. "Everything," she answered.

"Like what?" Angela wanted to know what was on Isaiah's little mind.

"Church girls are boring," Tina said laughing.

Angela rolled her eyes; she knew Tina was teasing her. "Do you like him?" she asked.

"No!" she quickly countered. "He is not even my kind of man,

I told you guys last night, I admire his personality nothing else. He is your kind of man anyway; Church boy and a Pastor's son." She smiled. "We do not have to date every guy we come in contact with, sometimes we should just enjoy the platonic relationships we have with that gender, and it can be refreshing and fun…" her eyes travelled to the gown that Angela had laid on the bed "… wait, is that what you want to wear?" "A gown" Angela responded to her.

"Why do you always wear loose clothes?" Tina asked her cousin.

"I do not always wear loose clothes" Angela countered "But they are comfortable anyway," Angela said, she brought out her flat shoes.

"Even sister Rita wears sexy clothes," Tina said. Angela dressed just like her grandma, and she had no problem with that at all.

Angela picked up a pillow and playfully used it to head the back of Tina's head.

"I change my mind; I'm going to dress up," Tina said and ran out of Angela's room. Angela laughed and shook her head.

Around 8:30 a.m. The four women were on the way to church. The drive to church seemed longer because grandma Peaches kept hammering on a particular topic that had made Angela bother for days. "I cannot wait to watch my granddaughters settle down with the man of their dreams." She said. Grandma Peaches and Angela were seated at the back while Ashley and Tina were in the front with Ashley driving.

"Grandma Peaches, you will have to wait for a little while because I Am Not Ready For Marriage!" She counted the last words.

"You will always be the one to oppose," Grandma told Tina.

"You are not ready for marriage because you are always seen with different men, we cannot even tell the difference between your platonic friends and your boyfriend." She attacked her with words. "I am single grandma Peaches, I currently have no time for man drama. I am just enjoying the gift of friendships and besides, you know the nature of my job involves me interacting with lots of people." She explained. "Get a real job, Tina." Grandma Peaches told her.

"Your idea of a real job is waking up every morning, wearing corporate and sticking your butt to a chair till the day is over. Wake up grandma this is the twenty-first century, the world has gone digital." She replied.

"Stop it you two, we are going to church." Ashley scolded them. "Anyways my dear" grandma Peaches turned to Angela "God created us in pairs, like I and your grandpa miller, your mom and your dad, you and your future husband.

Start working towards building meaningful relationships with men, I cannot wait for your wedding day." Grandma Peaches patted Angela on her back.

When they got to church, Angela felt her lips dry, she had forgotten to apply lip gloss so she excused herself to the bathroom. She met Isaiah in the hallway and thanked him for the gift she received from him through her cousin. "I wanted to give my gift in person, but it seemed you went in quite early," he said.

"I was tired, but "thank you!" she said as she walked to the bathroom.

After the praise and worship program, Pastor Brown called all single men and women and prayed for them. "We need many weddings in this Church" he said. It was as if the Holy Spirit had ministered in his heart the conversation Angela and her family had on their way to church.

"Amen." The congregation chorused.

After service, Michelle proposed an invite to Angela, "We have to hang out and catch up like the old times during the week.

What'd you say?" Michelle was Angela's childhood best friend and the only friend she had left in this town, they had kept in contact even when Angela was away. Weeks passed and Angela still hadn't called Charles even though she knew that she promised him that she would call, she was still embracing the serenity of being back home after so many years. From time to time, members of the church came in on few occasions to visit Angela; some went with gifts like sweat shirts, boxes of muffins, pie and puddings. She was admired by lots of people and many parents wanted their children to associate with her. She was thinking of going back to the choir but some parents had encouraged her to join the children ministry to serve. She decided that she was going to pray about it and let God direct her to the service unit where she will function most and be more impactful. She was so occupied that she completely forgot that Charles had given her his number to call him when she came back to town.

The following week, one fateful morning Angela was still asleep when grandma Peaches entered her room. "You are still sleeping?" she exclaimed! Angela murmured into the pillow, she didn't know why grandma Peaches always made a fuss about her sleeping till this time, it wasn't like she had anything to do nor anywhere to go but grandma Peaches would always say a virtuous woman should wake up on time and make her home. When she saw how reluctant it was for Angela to stand up, she walked over to the window and opened the curtains. "Grandma Peaches, the lights!" She shouted!

"it is a symbol that the day has begun Angela, Proverbs chapter 6 verses 10 and eleven." *it was the bible verse that said "a little sleep, a little slumber, a little folding of the hands to sleep: so shall thy poverty come as one that travelleth, and thy want as an armed man.* It had become her wake up alarm from grandma Peaches since she came back home.

"Grandma Peaches, it is not like I have a job or anywhere to go yet" She pouted.

"These came for you." She threw three envelopes on the bed. "That is why you have to wake up on time and start applying for jobs."

"I do grandma Peaches, I do! The few I have applied for, I haven't gotten any replies." She explained to her grandma as she opened the first envelope. "Oh my goodness!" she opened her eyes wide. "Grandma, I love you, please hug me." She said excitedly as she pulled her frail grandmother into a tight hug. Grandma Peaches did not fully understand what was

happening, before she could ask, Angela gave her the clarity she was looking for. "I got a job!" she screamed, "Hired fulltime position as a financial assistant, the company will pay twenty-one dollars per hour, healthcare and other benefits also included." She read out loud.

"Woo hoo!" grandma Peaches shouted. Ashley and grandpa miller hurried down, "what happened?" Ashley asked.

"Angela has gotten a job." She announced excitedly.

"Congratulations!" her grandpa congratulated her and left almost immediately but Ashley went further into the room to hug her daughter and congratulate her.

"What is in the other envelope?" grandma Peaches asked Angela who quickly picked it up and tore the envelope open. "It's a rejection letter from another company," she said sadly.

"Don't think about it, baby girl. Be grateful for the job you have now. When are you resuming?" Ashley asked her.

"On Monday." Angela looked at the letter to confirm.

"I pray you don't sleep till 10o'clock on that day." Grandma Peaches remarked.

"Grandma!" Angela sulked.

"I am glad you got this job baby, now that you will be going out every day, maybe you will finally meet someone to start a decent relationship with," Grandma said while walking out of her room.

This brings Angela, back to the thoughts of getting a man and building a relationship. "Maybe lord, just maybe." But then, she thanked God for another significant milestone in her life, she was thrilled because a bright future was ahead of her. On Monday, Angela resumed work. Her grandma practically walked her to the driveway and reminded her how she used to walk her to the school bus when she was younger. Angela blushed. "The lord is good, hallelujah" grandma Peaches said.

"All the time," Angela affirmed.

"Congratulations on your new career my darling." Grandma Peaches felt proud. "Smart work pays off."

"Welcome aboard" the general manager welcomed Angela.

"Thank you, "she answered.

He took her to the conference room and introduced her to the members of staff.

"We need more young blood here," the human resource manager said. Looking around, there weren't many young people in the company. After the introduction, everyone clapped their hands to welcome Angela. The receptionist; Beatrice walked up to her and invited her for girls outing they called "Happy Hours" every Friday evening but she quickly denied the offer politely. She did not want to rush into anything

especially making friends. She wanted to define her relationships and not mix personal lives with work. Two men were 'drooling' on her one of them asked her out on the weekend, but she said no. Even though Angela was keen on meeting someone ad starting out a relationship, she wanted to be careful, she had standards. She always thought to meet someone at church or at least someone who was invested in

Christ. "God will bring a man who has the same faith as mine." She thought to herself. Going to work during the weekdays,

Saturday and Sunday, she was busy with church activities. When she received her first salary, she paid her tithe to God and got gifts for everyone in the house including her best friend Michelle. Grandma Peaches told her not to spend all her money on them and forget that she had to take care of herself and also save up for a rainy day. Angela insisted that it was her first salary and she needed to give her loved ones a treat and she could start saving from her next salary.

CHAPTER FIVE

WORLDLY STANDARDS

That weekend, she went over to Michelle's home to visit her. She hadn't visited her since she got married, Michelle married the love of her life in her third year in college, and Angela could not attend because she had exams that period. Michelle was her first friend to get married and even then, she didn't feel pressured because her top priority was her education, grandma Peaches told her everything will fall into place in God's timing and so she has been waiting fervently for God's time to come. "Welcome to my home" Michelle welcomed Angela as she walked inside the sitting room, "this is your first visit since I got married and since you came back, we haven't had enough time to catch up. Sit." She offered

Angela a seat. Michelle and Angela talked about old times, how they were both active in the choir, did everything together, they were like sisters until she left town but nonetheless, they kept communicating. It pained Angela a lot that she could not make it to the wedding.

"So tell me about your boyfriend," Michelle asked Angela raising a brow.

"Michelle, you know me better, if I get a boyfriend, I think you will be one of the first persons to find out. I am waiting on God."

"Waiting on God?" she asked sarcastically, "is God going to descend the man from heaven? Angela, you went to college and for four years, you didn't go on a single date, yet you say you are waiting on God?"

"Michelle, you know how grandma Peaches can be, she told me not to and you know she is my closest guardian. She always said take it one step at a time, your first priority should be your education, a relationship and marriage will follow suit."

"Grandma Peaches is how old again?" Michelle asked Angela.

"Besides, you were the one who told me yourself that grandma Peaches had been married twice before she ended up with papa miller."

Angela became quiet.

"Even your grandma has had her fair share of men in her young age. We are church girls, we love God with our hearts but we also have to be smart."

"Michelle, I don't know. I am just being careful, guys of nowadays do not want to engage their selves in Godly

relationships, I am still waiting on that guy that will understand God's instructions and will keep our relationship pure until our wedding night."

Michelle scoffs. "I understand you my dear, but do you think that even the men you see in church are that pure?" "I know that not all of them are that clean, not even the reverend's son, but at least, in the midst of many, you found one…"

"… and who said we didn't have sex before marriage?"

Michelle cut her

"Did you?" Angela asked with uncertainty. She had told Michelle that she wanted to keep herself holy and sanctified until her wedding nights, they had both fantasized on how romantic and awkward it will be, she didn't know that Michelle got carried away with the things of the world.

"Couple of times," Michelle answered with a sly smile. "I know I didn't tell you this upon the fact that we talk all the time but it was because I knew that you will not understand, and you will be judgmental. So I had to keep it to myself."

"Michelle!" Angela called. "You just called me judgmental."

"You know I always say the truth, baby girl."

"Sexual sin is the only sin recorded in the bible as sinning against one's own body."

"We are married now, aren't we? Does that count now? Besides, but it is not the only sin, the bible also recorded that sin is sin; Lying, covetousness, backbiting and the rest." Michelle asked Angela. "Grandma Peaches is just trying to push down on you the kind of life she imagined or wished to have lived in her young age but she should let you learn some things on your own, make some mistakes and pick up the pieces. Even after marrying three different men, is her life bad? Is God not good to her?"

Angela became quiet; a part of her felt like Michelle was saying the truth. She had seen how life was in college but she continued being faithful.

As they were talking, Angela got a text on her phone from Karen "he proposed!" Karen was the pastor's daughter who wasn't even bothered about kissing her boyfriend in front of the school on convocation day. Her boyfriend has finally proposed to her after college and she who was just a faithful Christian who carried the bible on her head has found love. When she got home, she engaged Tina in a conversation.

"Low key, I regret not starting a relationship before I went to college." She told Tina "Why?" She asked.

"Because maybe I won't meet any man in my life," she answered.

"Why do you say so?" Tina stopped peeling the cucumber she was peeling.

"It is how I feel." She answered calmly.

"Feelings are not facts" Tina answered her. "You chose not to engage in any relationship throughout the school. You came back a few weeks ago, it is not like you are thirty-five so why are you so worried, you are not supposed to let anyone pressure you, take your time and lean on God's time it will surely happen." Angela asked Tina that aside from consistent prayers and sitting back to wait on God, what she can do to get men's attention. Tina smiled, she did not expect such a question from Angela but she answered her nonetheless and gave her an honest reply. "You need a total makeover, change your hair, let go of some of your grandma gowns, smile often and be more approachable." She answered.

"There is nothing wrong with my face and my hair and besides, those gowns are very comfortable, you should try them." "You are impossible" Tina rolled her eyes.

"Listen, Angela, you cannot get a man if you do not put yourself out there. You are either at work, church or home. You do not have any other friend aside from Michelle, whenever you go grocery shopping grandma Peaches is always by your side like your boyfriend. Because you have thick beautiful natural hair, you have refused to go to the salon and thanks to technology, you order for stuff online too." Angela was attentive.

"You need to go on dates, as many as you can. You do not have to sleep with them. Go enjoy lunch, dinner, and movies you can even visit the parks, engage in intelligent discussions and know these men properly. Your idea of a perfect date still exists but then the world is evolving and this is how it is being done now." "Thank you" Angela managed to voice out.

"I repeat, do not sleep with anyone. Everyone knows you are a virgin, keep yourself if you are determined to, and do not let anyone intimidate you or talk you down. Be calm as a dove and wise as a serpent, even the bible tells you so." Tina reiterated. She knew how gullible Angela was and she did not want her to misinterpret everything she had advised her to do and begin to blame herself in the end.

"Grandma Peaches will want me to bring all my dates home."

"Don't listen to grandma. She is old school, which is why we always seem to argue."

"Thank you for this." Angela appreciated what Tina had told her, she stood up and walk towards her room. When she got to her room, she lay down on her bed and began to review her conversation with her two closest friends Michelle and Tina.

They both had similar ideas with slight differences. How was grandma Peaches going to cope with the changes she was about make? One thing that is constant in life is change and it wasn't as if she will grow into a bad girl, she just wanted to adjust to fit in more. "This is my life and I will take charge of it" were her last words before she drifted off to sleep for the night.

CHAPTER SIX

IS HE THE ONE

Charles on the other hand had come back home, he rented a one-bedroom apartment and moved Stephanie and his son from her parent's house. He had applied for jobs since he came back but hadn't gotten any substantial reply yet. He was really determined in changing his lifestyle for the sake of his son, but the streets were calling him, it was pulling him harder than he had thought it would. When he came back from college, he spent the money he had managed to save on getting the new apartment, paying for his son's daycare, setting up the new house and sorting out some utility bills. He was a college graduate and couldn't bring himself down to doing menial jobs. He was silently praying that he gets called for a job soon. Charles was even more frustrated because he felt like.

Stephanie did not understand him and she did not want to.

She kept on demanding stuff because she felt he had money.

Charles had thought that the expenses on him would reduce because she had a job but it did not. He made a mental note to sit her down and talk to her about their situation when he got home from grocery shopping. As he pulled over at the car park, he spotted a familiar face, someone he didn't want to know that he was back in town; since he came back, he had tried his best to keep a low profile. He rolled up his window and decided to wait until the person was out of the parking lot. His phone rang, it was Stephanie, and he picked it up. "What's up?" he answered the phone.

"Are you done grocery shopping?" she asked.

"Are you ok Stephanie? I left the house less than fifteen minutes ago."

"Well, I just wanted to tell you to get some medicine for baby Leo when you are done, I will text their names to you."

"O..." before he could complete his word, someone knocked loudly on his window. It frightened him. He looked up and saw who it was; it was an old friend, someone he had known in the streets before he went to college.

"Are you crazy man?" Charles yelled! As he rolled down his window, "do not creep up on people that way."

"Long time no see" Ricky greeted him with a big smile.

Charles rolled the glass back up and came out of the car. "I'm not happy to see you rick, why did you creep up on me that way?"

"I'm sorry man" Ricky apologized.

"Welcome back from college, so you got a degree now" Ricky shook hands with Charles.

"Yes man, got a degree in computer engineering, put some respect to my name, and don't approach me making a scene like that next time."

"Bad guy, so you don't need the streets no more?" Ricky asked Charles.

"I'm a new person, leave man; I'm a brand-new man," Charles replied, refusing to be intimidated by his own decision; he looked Ricky straight in the eye. Charles kept on looking at him and thinking he looks like a mess, he wasn't just selling drugs, he was also taking them.

"I need a favor from you man."

Charles knew the kind of personality his friends from the street had, it was either he wanted to beg for a couple of boxes or he wanted some new contacts. Either way, he did not have some money to spare neither was he ready to let go of the contacts he had because if Ricky gets screwed up, he will snitch up, on him. "What do you want?" he asked.

"You know I've got no degree and as it is, I am having a hard time sorting my bills. I tried, I tried my best, I even got a job at McDonald's, it wasn't easy, the job was beneath me because I do not want any freaking person talking down on me or looking down on me…"

"What kind of job do you want Ricky? You only have a high school degree," only God knows if you graduated with good grades Charles said to himself, "you landed a 9 to 5 job at McDonald's, you are not in the street risking your life every day and you think people looking down on you is a problem? So you rather have no job than work at McDonald's?" Charles asked Ricky emphasizing the word MCDONALDS.

"Look man, all I wanted to ask was if you can help me get on some stuff and if you do not want to go that path, you can give me some connections and I will just get back on my feet, and make a little money."

"Ricky man, you know I'm out of the game, I now have a child and I am trying to build my life so if I'm going to even help you, I do not want my name on your lips, I do not want to go to prison because you were slinging something on the street.

If anything happens, you do not have anything to lose but I have a family, don't become an informant and do not use my name because you will pay for it."

"Does that mean that you will help me? Will you give me your contacts now that you are out of the game?" Charles stepped forward really fast and snatched him up by the middle of his shirt and squeezed him really tight, He lifted him off the ground up to the same height as himself.

"Put me down man" Ricky orders. "Do not mess with a man who

has nothing to lose, I got you, take my word and put me down."

"Since I came back from school, I have been trying to keep myself on a low, do not bring my leg out" Charles warned as he dropped him down.

"I almost got shot last week. I was at the store trying to buy some bologna and bread with some couple of beer, there was a scene and everyone got distracted, I grabbed the two beers and put them underneath my shirt, the guy behind the counter was an Iranian guy, I never knew he would be able to tell before I knew it, he jumped behind the counter and pulled out a gun.

It was so bad other customers thought I was a serious criminal who had come to rip the shop of all her money. He asked me to drop the beer and every other thing I had bought and asked me never to come to his shop again. he said he knew me on the streets and he always noticed me when I came to the shop to buy chips and if I was hungry, all I needed to do was to ask, I am always here, helping people but going into my freezer to get my cans of

bologna, I have no respect for you, don't come in here because if

you steal something as small as a piece of candy,

I will blow your head off!"

Charles just stood, looking at him in disgust.

"I could not believe what happened, I had never been this low in

my entire life, it was even more demeaning than working in old

McDonalds and I do not ever want to be in that position again,

that's why I am asking that you help me, so I can save up enough

to at least attend a technical college and get a degree of my own.

However, I'm hearing that most people are not honoring technical

colleges anymore."

"I don't know man, I'm hearing that for most jobs you need to have

a college degree, but there are still places hiring people who have

trades. Ricky you can gain experience and get on the job training and create a name for yourself. I'm just saying think about it man, I got to go, you have kept me in front of this grocery store long enough. I really need to get something."

As Charles walked towards the door of the store, Ricky tried to enter with him but Charles stopped him. "I hope this wasn't the store you stole from?" I do not want to be seen with you or affiliated with you in public, I'm still trying to walk on a new slate, go home, and I will gather some contacts and get back to you.

Charles walks into the store to get the groceries; he bought some supplies that will be needed in the house. When he was done, he walked to the counter to pay for the things he had picked.

"Two hundred and fifty dollars ma'am" the cashier told the lady standing he was currently attending to. She opened her purse and brought out some cash and the cashier packaged her goods and handed it to her. The lady seemed very familiar but he couldn't figure out who the person was, as she turned, he saw her face and a wide smile crept to his lips. "Angela!" Angela looked up and saw Charles, she hadn't completely forgotten to call him but then, any time she remembered, something else would take her attention away, besides she had started her new job and did not always have time on her hands.

"Hey Charles, long time no see." She smiled back then face palmed herself. "I'm sorry."

"You promised."

"I know. I will make it up to you. I have to run; my lunch break is almost over." She said hurriedly.

"Not so fast. This time, give me your contact; I will be the one to place a call" he raised one eyebrow and handed her his phone. She quickly typed her phone number on it, gave Charles a quick hug and rushed out of the store. Charles paid for his own groceries and went to the pharmacy store to get drugs that Stephanie had asked him to buy for their son.

That evening, Charles called Angela on the phone. "What's up Angela?"

"Hello, Charles. Good evening." The phone was silent for a while before Charles broke the silence. He was never a man of few words when it came to women. Charles was able to date a lot of girls in college despite knowing the fact that he had been joined together in holy matrimony with the mother of his son, but when it came to Angela, he was tongue twisted. Whether it was because of the fact that he genuinely liked her or because she was grandma Peaches granddaughter or even because she has these scrutinizing eyes that she used to gaze upon him, he didn't know. He could literally picture her as they were on the phone. "So, how has it been since you came back?" he managed to say.

"It hasn't been completely easy, but it has been fun. Reunited with my old town, living in my childhood bedroom again, the church has been amazing and I got a job as a financial assistant. Is God not good?" Angela who was lying down on her bed got up slowly and made her way to her study chair and table. She sat on the chair and raised her legs on the table. "What about you?" she asked him.

"It hasn't been easy, still trying to get a job; I've been trying to sort out some mess I left behind…"

"Oh Charles, what kind of mess did you get yourself into?" Angela asked him. When they attended school together, she knew him as a quiet and less troublesome boy that could easily be intimidated. She was like an elder sister to him even though she knew he was older than her by a few months. "No big deal. Well, I called to know when you will actually be free to hang out with me."

"I don't know, for now, I have work on Mondays to Fridays, then on weekends, I do my laundry, grocery shopping and church." She told him.

"So you cannot make one weekend for me?"

"That is why I said I do not know for now," she said emphasizing the last two words.

"Ok, how about one of these days, after work?" he suggested.

"Wednesdays and Fridays, I have weekly activities to attend in church."

"Monday, Tuesday, Thursday? Don't make this hard for us little Peaches." He said. Angela wanted to give him a tough time, she was worth it anyway so he will be patient with her, it wasn't like she was used to this kind of life, going out on dates, talking to guys and the rest, he believed that with time, he will help her adapt. He was still on the phone outside the house when he noticed Stephanie came out, carrying their son in her arms, she was walking in his direction.

"You know what Angela? We will continue this conversation later, I got to go now."

Before she could bid him farewell, he hung up. Such an urgency she thought, maybe it was really important. She stood up from the chair she was sitting and went back to her bed. Is he the

one Lord? Should I give Charles a chance?

CHAPTER SEVEN

LET'S MAKE THIS WORK

What are you doing outside?" Stephanie asked when he got to where he was standing, "who were you talking to?" baby Leo stretched his hand for his father to carry him, and Charles put his phone into his pocket and took him from Stephanie. He had been absent in his son's life for his first five years and had been doing his best to make up for it since he came back.

"Nothing, no one." He said incoherently. "How is he doing, is he better now?" he asked her.

"Yes, his fever has reduced." She used the back of her palm to touch his forehead to check his temperature.

"Let's go inside, it's getting cold." Charles started to walk towards their patio.

"I want us to talk," she told him as she fastened her pace to meet up with him.

"Well, let's get inside first." He answered her without even looking in her direction.

When they got inside, Charles put on the television and set it on a cartoon channel for baby Leo to watch.

"You said you want to talk." Charles sat opposite her in their little sitting-room consisting of two small couches and a love seat, a small television and a shelf and their old baby cot. "Yeah, well I know we got together under an uncomfortable circumstance before you went to college. Charles since you came back, we have been leaving as just housemates joined together because of our son. If I had my way, I wouldn't have let my parents force me into this kind of marriage because it is not what I planned for myself either.

We are already together, so instead of living like strangers in our matrimonial home, let us make this work; for baby Leo, for my sanity, for your happiness, for our parents. I promise to support you and always be by your side no matter what happens, I love you Charles, and you know I really do." By the time she was done talking, streaks of tears were already flowing down her cheeks. She had thought this over and over again since Charles came back from college and decided to talk to him about it. Since he came back, they hadn't even shared a kiss, the time she tried to kiss him, he quickly removed his face and acted as if nothing happened. Stephany felt embarrassed even though it was just the two of them. They had several minor misunderstandings especially because Charles was always on edge with her, when it came to Stephanie, he was always impatient.

Charles heaved a sigh. "Stephanie I'm sorry if I have made you feel uncomfortable, since I came back, I've had so many things on my mind and it hasn't been easy as the man that I have become.

I have been thinking about providing, and caring for you. This is a family and we have to survive. I really do ….."

"…that is why you have me, I promise to support you." She cut him off. She knew he was going to come up with some lame excuse of being too focused on building their relationship will derail him from making money to give them financial stability. It wasn't the first time he wanted to use that card on her. One time when he was in college, she accused him of cheating on her because for a whole month, he did not call her to check up on her nor their son. He got angry and told her that it was not easy being in college, footing his own bills and taking care of her and their son, so he needed to focus. She felt like she understood him and gave him the benefit of the doubt, but she was determined never to let Charles slip up on her before the worse could happen. What is the worse that could happen, filing for a divorce after her parents die? They were literarily the ones who orchestrated this whole marriage idea. How she wished they had let her become a single mom as long as Charles was taking responsibility for the child, she knew she would have found someone who will love her genuinely. At the initial stages, she was angry at the innocent baby for coming into the world but as he began to grow, all her anger and hatred vanished when she looked into her son's blue eyes or when he smiles just like his father. Her most memorable moments were when he was first learning how to talk. She was glad she did not miss any of those moments in her son's life. Even though Charles did not love Stephanie, he did not want to hurt her, she was the mother of his son and he had respect for her. Seeing her cry broke him, he did not want to be the villain in the relationship "stop crying Stephanie, I have heard you, we will make it work." He said just to calm her down even though he knew that he did not mean it. She stood up and sat on his lap. "I love you, Charles, I love you." She told him. Charles used his thumb to clean the tears on her face. Inside of her, she was glad that she finally had the courage to talk to Charles about what had been bothering her since he came back from college. She drew her face closer to him and waited for a reaction from him, none.

Then she placed her lips on his. She kissed him for a few seconds before he began to reciprocate it. He wrapped his arms around her waist to support her, pulled away from the kiss and said, "Stephanie, we cannot do this in front of baby Leo."

He tried to make her come down. "Then, let us go inside, he will fall asleep while watching the cartoon." Charles gave a disapproving look. "Please Charles," she whimpers "it's been so long, make me feel like a woman again." She pleaded. Charles stood up and carried her inside their bedroom to make love to her.

CHAPTER EIGHT

OH NO!

Weeks after weeks, Angela finally agreed to meet up with Charles after work. He picked her up at her office and drove her to a local restaurant for dinner. "I just want us to eat first; you have been at work all day. I hope you do not mind the scenery?" he asked referring to the fact that the restaurant wasn't too classy or exquisite. He did not want to over impress her, he knew she didn't care about it and besides, he was not working yet, and it was all he could afford comfortably. "Thank you." She said as he drew out a chair for her to sit. After a few minutes, a beautiful slim waitress hanging a towel over her shoulder came to take their orders. They sat down and conversed about their day before the food came. Charles told her that he was still searching for jobs and most of the companies he had applied for had either not replied to him or the ones who had replied would say they currently did not need graduate interns, but wanted computer engineers with years of working experience, however when they do, they will email him. His patience was running thin. She told him about her job, what she does in the office, how tasking it has been and how she had been able to adapt. Their food came and they ate quietly. Angela noticed some awkward stares from some other customers towards her way, but she assumed it was all in her mind. What did she have with them that would make them look at her as if she had stolen something?

After the meal, they left. He took her to a flower garden as they admired the different vegetation. "God is indeed wonderful in his creation." She smiled as she looked at them in awe. "Yes, he is." He replied quietly.

Angela brought out her phone and took some pictures of the

flowers; she also gave her phone to Charles to take some pictures of her with them. She quickly changed her phone wallpaper and they both went to sit down on a bench.

She noticed Charles who was quite chatty earlier had grown so quiet. "What is happening?" she asked him. "Is there something worrying your mind?"

"Yes Angela, it is you." He used his palm to rub his face. Angela was still confused; she did not know what she had done to

Charles in the space of a few hours to make him grow so quiet.

"What did I do?" she asked him as she fluttered her long lashes nervously.

"I like you, can't you see?"

Angela was taken aback by his confession, yes she expected it, she knew it was going to come to that, but she did not expect him to bring it up on their first date, she wanted a more traditional kind of dating when they have to go on a couple of dates, then he will make his intentions known, he will see her family and they will start their courtship. That was the picture grandma Peaches always painted for her, "a man who loves you genuinely will have no issues meeting your family first

before starting a courtship with you, and it proves his intentions are pure."

"Charles…"

"You do not have to say anything right now, I just wanted you to know how I feel, how much I care about you, since sophomore year. When I saw you again after a few years at your graduation, I realized how I feel about you. But if you want to take your time to think about it, then it is fine."

Angela gave a nod. "You need to rest, let me drop you home." When they got to where Charles had parked his car, he opened the passenger's door for her to enter and sit then turned around and opened the driver's side and sat down. "I really enjoyed my time with you, Angela." Angela smiled before Charles hooked his seat belt. He quickly leaned over and brought his face close to Angela's face. She became nervous, should she stop him? She thought or should she let him go ahead, she was a few seconds away from having her first kiss. Charles paused and waited for a reaction; he expected her to say something or push him away but when he got none, he went ahead and

pressed his lips against her for a feathery kiss, slightly parting her lips to make way for his lips to fit in. Angela just relaxed and closed her eyes, experiencing what it felt like to be kissed and savoring every moment. She did not even know what to do, should she move her lips also? Or just sit down and let him continue? She thought to herself. After a few seconds, Charles pulled away and sat down on his seat and hooked his seat belt. He huffed and said, "That was the best six seconds of my life." Put the car keys in its ignition and the engine roared to life. He drove her home before going back to his family. He began to feel like he was living two different lives. When Angela finally agrees to be his, what will happen with Stephanie? He knew he was definitely going to find a way to explain to her that he has a son out of wedlock. "Where have you been?" Grandma Peaches asked Angela when she got into the house. "I was just hanging out with a friend grandma." She replied as she walked over to her grandma and gave her a kiss on her cheeks. "Good evening grandpa." She greeted her grandpa who was sitting next to his wife grandma Peaches. "I know I want you to go all out and meet new people, start dating and bring me a grandson-in-law but you have to do it the right way." She warned Angela. Angela knew what she meant by doing things the right way. "Do not be unequally yoked with an unbeliever" grandma Peaches said to her. Bring him home let us assess him. "Yes, grandma Peaches" Angela

answered. She quickly ran into her room. She thought of calling

Tina her cousin to tell her she had finally had her first kiss with Charles, but she decided against it. She was overwhelmed with what had transpired between her and Charles and wanted to share but with someone who will not judge her rather understand how she felt so she picked up her phone and called

Michelle.

"Hey Angela, what's up?" she asked.

"I'm good." She paused. "So I went on a date today and had my first kiss." She blurted out.

"No way, tell me about it."

Angela took her time to explain to Michelle about the whole situation with Charles, how he had gone for her graduation and how they bumped into each other at the store.

"Angela" Michelle paused and listened quietly intently to what Angela had to say.

"Yeah"

"I'm happy for you about the whole experience, but Charles is not the guy that you should be dealing with." Michelle broke the news to her.

"I don't understand." Angela became tensed, was telling Michelle a bad idea?

"You haven't been around for a while and I know no one must have told you but Charles is married."

"Oh no!"

CHAPTER NINE

THE TRUTH

Angela was starstruck; she did not believe what her ears had heard from her best friend Michelle. When did all this happen? She asked herself. Even though Charles was not quite the church boy, she had known him to be timid that she even had to stand up for him on some occasions. Charles was older than her by a few months, but she saw herself as his elder sister. She was very surprised when she saw him at her graduation; the way he looked, talked, his gestures, he had grown so matured and into a man but he did not look married, besides why would Charles be chasing after her if he was legally married with a child. Her head was in turmoil as she tried to process what Michelle had just told her, maybe she was referring to another Charles and not the Charles who had just

kissed her for her very first time, who unconsciously, she was already

developing butterflies for.

"Angela," Michelle called, but Angela was still lost in her thoughts.

"Angela!" she called louder.

"Yeah, I'm here" Angela replied absent-mindedly, she was

still trying to process all that she had heard.

"No, you are not. What was the last thing I said?"

Michelle questioned Angela.

"Hum, Charles is married?" she gave a question-like

answer.

"You were definitely not listening, we need to sit and talk.

There is so much to talk about."

"Ok then, I will call you when I'm free and we can talk.

Good night." Angela hung up the phone.

She needed to hear from the horse's mouth, she needed to talk to Charles, what was this all about? She opened her text messaging app and texted Charles. "We need to talk ASAP, call me when you get this text." she lightly tapped her phone on her head. She waited for a few minutes which felt like some hours and still no reply. She knew the text had been delivered; the delivery receipt had appeared on her phone. Was Michelle right after all? Time will tell. Angela had trouble sleeping that night and for the first time in a long time, she let her worries overcome her and she forgot to pray. Angela tossed and turned on her bed until she fell asleep. She had not even been able to catch enough sleep when her alarm blew off. *"Argh!"* she groaned as she used her left hand to silence the ticking alarm clock above her head, she forced herself to get up from the bed before grandma Peaches would come for her.

Her mood the previous night did not make her prepare her work outfit for the next day so she walked into her closet for something to wear. She took her bath, wore her clothes and applied light make-up on her face before going down for breakfast. Grandma Peaches her biggest fan was already in the kitchen preparing toasts and tea for Angela, she did that every morning since Angela started work. Sometimes, she will make oats and dice berries or apples in it, other times, it could be bacon or even a burrito but grandma always makes sure that Angela never leaves for work with an empty stomach. She did not have the appetite to eat anything but she knew grandma would be suspicious, so she pretended to have a meeting and asked grandma Peaches to package the food for her and she will eat it after her meeting when she got to work.

Honestly, Angela knew that she wouldn't be able to eat anything until she clarifies what Michelle told her about Charles. She did not even have time to check her phone until she got to work. "Good morning Angela" the receptionist greeted her with a bright smile. "Morning Beatrice" Angela replied warmly. She could not even reply to her with the cheerful smile she always gave her when she arrived at work in the morning. Angela got to her desk and set up her files then her phone rang. *Charles*, she picked up the phone almost immediately to answer the phone. "Hello." "What's up babe, I got your message last night," he answered anxiously. "Good morning to you too," she replied to him, pointing out his lack of courtesy.

"I am sorry, but you sounded so urgent on the phone." he defended.

"I sent you that text last night Charles, but you could not reply because you were with your wife." Angela blurted.

Charles was quiet. Angela waited for a few seconds but there was no reply, she removed the phone from her ears to check if Charles was still connected and he was. "Tell me I'm wrong," she said softly when she began to realize that her best friend might be correct after all.

"We really need to sit and talk Angela." was the only thing that came out of his mouth. Was she really ready to listen to everything he had to say? What will his explanations change if really, he is married? She was a devoted Christian and she frowned against adultery.

When she prayed for a spouse, she wanted her own man and not to share another woman's man. Grandma Peaches will never approve of that, it will break her heart. During lunch, Charles came to her office and offered to take her out for lunch. Angela was quiet most of the time, she barely ate her food, because all she needed was an answer or an explanation. If really he was married, when did he get married? What had happened? Who was the lady he tied the knot with? What were his intentions for her, knowing full well that he could never be hers? After lunch, they sat in his car. "Tell me that you have not taken an oath of for better and for worse?" Angela asked Charles. They were parked in front of her office building. "It's a long story babe; I hope you will listen to me. I never wanted any of this." his forehead creased, he was stressed. "So, what am I to you?" she looked at him with a piercing gaze. "A naive young woman you can trick into taking her innocence then dumping her when she is miserable?" Angela asked. "Don't say that, I have never thought of you that way and I never will,

I respect you, and you are beautiful, strong, God-fearing and hardworking. I always have had mad love for you, Angela, right from our school days, you have always been in my heart...." "...and yet you are married to another." she cuts him off "Circumstances beyond my control," he replied to her.

"Were you dragged to the altar with a rope on your neck?" she asked him. "She was pregnant," he confessed. Angela could not believe her ears, she had not fully come to terms with the fact

that Charles was married; he gave her a new revelation that he was already a father. "Any more surprises?" she asked, her eyes were watery. Charles took his time to explain everything to her, how he was forced to get married before going to college, he even told her how he felt like Stephanie had betrayed him. He suspected that she had either showed her mother the pregnancy test result or intentionally left it on the bed for her mother to see just to trap him. He knew she loved him more than he did her and she was just looking for ways to tie him down.

"Yes, I am married but I cannot stop thinking about you. You are special to me, I love you Angela, and you are the one in my heart." Charles continued to fill her head. "This is too much for me to take in at once, I need to go." she opened the car door and got out of the car and went into her office. She had the urge to cry and scream but she had to control herself, she was at her place of work.

Angela managed to fake a smile till her closing time, she got into her old corolla sports car and drove back home. She was thankful when she got into the house, she did not find anyone, and she was definitely not in the mood for chitchats. She walked into her bedroom, laid down on the bed and screamed into the pillow she cried until she felt like her eyes were going to bulge out. "Lord, is this your plan for me? I have been faithful," she kept on asking. After a while, she fell asleep. She woke to grandma Peaches towering over her; she opened her eyes slowly and felt dizzy. "You are burning up" grandma Peaches stated. "I was mad at you for not showing up to bible study and you were home only for me to come up here and see you covered up in bed!" Grandma Peaches pressed the back of her palm on Angela's forehead. "Here's the water and towel" Ashley presented them to grandma Peaches as she walked into the room. "What happened honey? Do you feel sick from work?" Ashley asked. Angela just nodded her head, she was scared that if she opened her mouth to talk, her voice might betray her and grandma Peaches and her mother Ashley would know what she had been up to since she got home. "I will prepare you my special recipe mushroom soup, it will make you feel better but you have to call in sick at work tomorrow, you will need all the rest that you can get." grandma Peaches told Angela and stood up. "Ashley, come join me in the kitchen so we can finish up on time." Ashley stood up from the edge of the bed she sat down after handing over the bowl of water and towel to grandma Peaches. "By the way, Isaiah asked about you today, he was concerned because you barely missed weekly activities." Ashley winked at her before finally leaving the room. Isaiah was the only son of Pastor Brown, the resident pastor of St. John's Baptist church, she was surprised about what her mother has said because aside from courtesy greetings, she and Isaiah barely said a word to each other.

Days passed and Angela refused to talk to Charles nor did she reply to his texts, she was hurt that he had kept such important information about himself from her until she had to find out herself. Michelle had been trying her best to contact her too but Angela found ways to avoid Michelle and the gist she had to bring, she had heard it all from the horse's mouth. Angela had called in sick at work and her boss asked her to take the remaining days of the week off for her to rest and recover.

CHAPTER TEN

MATCH MAKING

On Sunday after church, they were seated in the back of grandma Peaches car, while Ashley was in the front with Angela's cousin Tina, they were all chatting and laughing when grandma Peaches suddenly asked Angela, "What do you think about Isaiah?"

"What about him?" Angela answered the question by asking a question, she was quite unsure of what grandma

Peaches wanted to inquire about. "Is he cute?"

"Yes, ma'am, he is ok." She affirmed. "At least, he has all the young girls in church drooling all over him," she muttered under her breath. "Sorry?" grandma Peaches asked Angela, she couldn't make out her last words. Tina who had heard her faintly because she was sitting directly in front of Angela at the passenger's seat smiled to herself. "Nothing grandma" Angela shook her head feigning that she didn't know what grandma Peaches was asking about.

"If I were single and young like you..." she continued her conversation about Isaiah.

"...What will you do?" She cuts her off.

"Well, I really wish he marries you," grandma Peaches finally said her wish. Angela's heart began to race; she knew something was up when Ashley talked about him when they came back from bible study a few days ago. If only they knew that the only person who had managed to gain her heart romantically had also ripped it into pieces. She could not talk about it because she never told them about him from the onset and grandma Peaches was always big on bringing your men home for proper evaluation before courtship begins. Everyone will blame her for giving her heart to someone they had never met. "You are a smart woman," grandma Peaches praised her granddaughter "and you deserve a good and God-fearing man who will love and respect you just like pastor brown respects

Julie." Pastor Brown was the presiding pastor of St. John's Baptist church and Julie was his second wife. The pastor's first wife died a few years after Isaiah was born, two years after her death, he married Julie because he did not want his son to grow up without the presence of a mother in his life. He knew being a Pastor came with many responsibilities, and he could not handle bringing up a child on his own. After their marriage, God blessed them with a daughter "Isabelle." looking at the family from outside; you will never know that Julie was not the biological mother of Isaiah and that Isaiah and Isabelle are halfsiblings. Pastor Brown also loved and respected her so much. "I invited him over for dinner."

"Grandma!" Tina shouted.

"What?" Grandma Peaches adjusted her thick-rimmed spectacles. "This is the twenty-first century, do people still match make? Besides, did you speak with Angela before inviting him for dinner?"

Tina asked her grandmother. "Aunt Ashley, are you in on this two?" Tina asked Ashley.

"Well, mama and I spoke about it last night." Ashley tried to hide her smile. While all these conversations were going on, Angela was bored and uninterested but everyone assumed it was because she was not feeling too well. That evening Isaiah came to grandma Peaches house for dinner, grandma Peaches and Ashley had overdone their selves, the dining table was filled with different cuisines, "are we having a party?" Tina asked when she came downstairs with Angela. Grandma Peaches and Ashley had laden the table with French onion soup and potato, grilled whole chicken and salad, red velvet cake and brownies were also present on the table. "There is ice cream in the freezer." grandma Peaches announced. During their conversation, grandma Peaches asked Isaiah some questions about himself; what he studied at school, if he was interested in the ministry like his father, she also asked him some questions about his values, she did not fail to chip in to chip in some points for Angela with every response Isaiah gave. After they had eaten, grandma Peaches, Ashley and Tina left Angela and Isaiah to themselves to get to know each other better. "I am glad that you feel better now."

"Thank you." Angela smiled.

"Bible study felt empty without you, I was glad that you could make it to church today," he told her. They were never close friends even when they were younger and even after she came back to town so striking a conversation was not that easy for them, they had nothing much to say to each other. Isaiah was not too bothered; he believed in baby steps and that with time, they will find common grounds to communicate on. When my mom told me you asked after me, I was surprised. I never knew you will notice everyone from the piano stand." "Not everyone Angela, its just you." he corrected her. Angela smiled at Isaiah's response, so the pastor's son could actually flirt she thought to herself. They continued talking and he even urged Angela to go back to the choir because she was blessed with an angelic voice, just like her name. When Angela got tired and told Isaiah that she needed to rest and she was getting cold. Isaiah informed grandma Peaches that he wanted to go; she packaged some food for him to take to his parents. Isaiah said goodnight to Angela, they exchanged numbers and he left.

"So?" Grandma Peaches asked Angela when Isaiah had left. Ashley and Tina were not left out; they kept on looking at her with an enquiry eye.

"So what?" Angela smiled.

"What do you think of him?" Tina asked.

"Well, he is a nice guy and we will get to know ourselves more as time goes on." she gave them the answer they wanted. They cheered her on and encouraged her that hopefully, things will work out well between the both of them. Angela just smiled and went back to her room claiming she needed to rest. Isaiah was a good guy, no doubt but Charles was already in her heart.

Isaiah is the "take home to mama kind of man," he will be good for her but is that what her heart wanted?

CHAPTER ELEVEN

SURPRISES

The next day Angela resumed work, she looked so much better. Charles had stopped calling and texting because she was not replying to any of his calls or text. She missed him dearly but she kept on praying for God to give her the fortitude to fight the feelings she had already developed. She did not know how far she had fallen until she got hurt.

"Good morning." the receptionist greeted her with a bright smile. "It's nice to see that you are actually feeling better," she added. "Thank you, Beatrice," Angela responded. "I appreciate your checking up on me, I got your text, I just could reply at that moment, then later it escaped my mind" Angela explained."Oh, it's nothing." Beatrice the receptionist waved it off. "By the way, a package came in for you this morning," she informed

Angela.

"A package from who?" she inquired. She had not ordered anything, neither was she expecting anyone to send her any package.

"A man brought it" Beatrice smiled.

"Man?" Angela asked. She walked towards Beatrice's table. "Which man?"

"A tall man, about six feet tall, very handsome too with perfectly tanned skin." Beatrice winked.

Charles,

Beatrice brought the bouquet of red roses from under her table, accompanied by a box of chocolate with an envelope tagged to it.

Angela was taken aback and for a moment, she felt butterflies in her tummy. Charles had stopped calling her because he knew she will not respond so he resolved to another method.

"Thank you." she appreciated Beatrice and took her package to her office. "You are welcome, you have a good man."

I know it's hard to believe coming from me, but I want you to know that I love you and I will choose you over and over again, I'm sorry. - Charles.

She read the handwritten note carefully over and over and over again until the picture of the paper had been stored in her head that even though her eyes were closed, she could picture Charles's handwriting, the watermark and even the folded parts of the paper. She smiled but never called to say thanks or the package received. At the end of the day, almost everyone in the office had heard that Angela's man had brought her a package, thanks to Beatrice. She did not bother to defend herself nor explain to the people who approached her, they will think that she was just lying although; it made her feel special in front of the female workers. The next day, he ordered for lunch and had it delivered to her office, Beatrice called her to sign and receive her package. She did not even bother to ask who had sent it to be delivered because she knew who it was already. "You are so lucky," Beatrice commented. *If only she knew.* "Thanks," Angela replied and took her lunch to her office to consume. Charles had ordered spaghetti garnished with seafood and turkey wings. She smiled when she opened the food plate.

She ate to her satisfaction and still did not call the provider to appreciate. She was still fighting within herself if she should give him a listening ear. Meanwhile, the previous night Isaiah had called and they had talked for a few minutes. He asked her if she was chanced during the week for a date and she accepted.

She wanted to do anything within her physical power to get Charles out of her mind but she forgot the bible passage that says; *"for the weapon of our warfare are not carnal, but mighty through God to the pulling down of strongholds, casting down imaginations, and every high thing that exalteth itself against the knowledge of God, and bringing into captivity every thought to the obedience of Christ."* 1 Corinthians 10 verses 4 and 5. That evening, Charles sent her a goodnight text and impulsively, she replied "thanks." Charles felt ecstatic that she finally replied to him. He knew that sooner or later he will have to tell her the whole truth but he wanted her to love him first. They live in a small town where one's business is everyone's business and it will have been hard to conceal the truth for a long time. Charles and Stephanie finally had an understanding with their selves, Stephanie learnt to support their home with the little income she was earning from the cafe she was working at, but it wasn't substantial because Charles's savings was running out. He decided to go back to the street to make some money. If he was not getting called for any job, he could just set up a small office where he will help people fix their computers. But it was capital intensive so he went back to selling drugs to be able to provide for his family, impress Angela and set up his business. He tried to be discreet when dealing with

Angela because he did not want Stephanie to find out, he did not want a situation whereby he will be summoned by their parents and questioned why he was defying his marriage vow, something he had never kept.

He was so happy after Angela replied to his goodnight message with a simple "thanks" the previous night, so he decided to pay her a surprise visit at her workplace.

"Hello ma'am, someone is here for you," Beatrice spoke into the phone after Charles requested to see her.

"Name please," Angela answered.

"Charles Wood," Beatrice said softly.

Angela felt her heart drop to her stomach, what was he thinking coming to look for her in the office? What if someone knew about his marital status around here?

"I am coming down." she dropped her pen and went to meet

Charles. A sensual smile appeared on Charles's lips as she made her way down the office stairs. She was looking more like a woman in her corporate gown, her hair laid with one side tucked behind her ears, exposing the glitter of her silver stud earrings. "You are so beautiful," he said when she got to him. "Let's talk outside," she told him and continued walking outside, she did not even smile back neither did she even pause to exchange pleasantries.

Charles followed her immediately, he opened the car door for her and she entered.

"You shouldn't have come here, what if someone knows about you?" she asked him harshly.

"What will you have me do?" I tried my best.

"What do you want?"

"Just hear me out Angela," he begged, when he saw that she stopped making a fuss, he continued.

"I'm going to get a divorce. I'm going to marry you. I love you so much and you mean more than anything in this world to me, just give me time, please." he explained.

"How much time?" she asked him.

"Enough time to tell Stephanie that it is no longer working." He used his palm to rub his face.

Even Angela could not believe the next words that came out of her mouth. "Fine! But we have to be discreet about this," she said with a straight face, looking forward.

"Thank you! Thank you!" Charles thanked her. He wanted to rush and hug her but she reminded him that his car windows were not tinted and they needed to be discreet.

CHAPTER TWELVE

FELT LIKE FILTH

Time passed, Angela and Charles continued their relationship. Every time they met or drove out of town, Angela would feel guilty, she would remember that he had a wife and son at home, but then she would comfort herself with the fact that he didn't love her and he was going to divorce her soon. *"If it's not me, it could be someone else, either way, he will still cheat."* she will say to herself just to make her feel better. She also continued seeing Isaiah, on their first date; Tina came home with bags of used synthetic hair. She could not afford to buy new hair. "I want to braid your hair," she told Angela. "Do you have a crochet needle?" she asked her.

"Hell no, I like to keep my hair natural." She said and sleeked her hair backwards.

"Hell yes! You are my cousin and I love you and I love your natural hair but sometimes, you need to change hairstyles, and Look different; it brings out your beauty from different angles."

"I will pass" Angela replied, in all honesty, she was protecting her scalp from dandruff, she knew hair extensions will increase the possibility of it coming.

"Get me a needle!"

"Where? You know I do not have any." She told Tina.

"Go to the beauty store then. These are things you are supposed to have."

Angela was a little bit upset; she did not like leaving the house especially when she did not plan to go anywhere that Saturday morning. She went to grandma Peaches bedroom and came back holding something in her hand. "Here is the needle." She handed it over to Tina.

"I am going to do light makeup on your face," Tina told her. "But it is Isaiah I am going out on a date with. He has seen me countless times without makeup in church." Angela argued.

"He has seen you countless times without makeup in

church, but not on a date, it is different."

"Well Grandma said I can wear her pearl beads," Angela told Tina. Tina almost choked on the water she was drinking.

"C'mon, do you want to wear grandma Peaches beads? You have graduated from the maxi gowns." She asked her cousin while laughing. "I have a rhinestone jewel set," she went to the bedroom and brought her a set.

"Thank you," Angela said as she was grateful for her stylish cousin.

With the help from stylish Tina, Angela had an up do hairstyle, rhinestone necklace, earrings, and bracelet. Her body was wrapped in a beautiful black dress and leopard skin high heels.

She looked beautiful, and she was ready to go for her date.

Angela was surprised with whom and what she had become, she tried her best to keep her relationship with Charles discreet by introducing Isaiah to her family as the one she was dating. At times when Isaiah and she would plan for a date, Charles will call and she will cancel on Isaiah then lie that she was working overtime. There were times she would even sneak out of the house at night just to go clubbing with Charles, then on Sunday, she will sit in a choir seat and minister with them. She was living a double life.

But there is nothing that will be done under the sun that cannot be revealed. Grandma Peaches began to notice slight changes in her character. She called Angela to talk to her, but she denied seeing someone else other than Isaiah. That night, Angela thought to herself that her grandma was becoming too inquisitive and she needed to be independent. She needed to be free to make her decisions, she thought of moving out and staying on her own. Angela found it difficult to raise the topic that she wanted to move out of her family house.

She knew grandma Peaches will disapprove and that was the more reason why she found it impossible to talk. She was going to say her mind anyway. It is better to try and get rejected than not trying at all than wishing one had tried anyway.

Saturday evening, after choir practice, Isaiah offered to drop Angela at home. Isaiah had informed Pastor Brown and Julie that he was courting Angela and they were very happy about it. While the family was eating dinner, Angela was not her usual self. She was quiet with a lot of thoughts. Sometimes grandma Peaches will make a joke then Ashley and Tina will burst into a fit of laughter but Angela did not react because her mind had drifted away. "Something wrong with you today?" grandma Peaches asked.

"No, ma'am," she said and looked down, tears rolled down her plump cheeks.

"Oh, my baby, why the tears, are you sick again?" Her grandma showed more concern.

"No."

"Did Isaiah do something to hurt you?" Ashley asked.

Tina stood up and went to her to comfort her.

"No, he did not." She answered blandly.

"So what bothers you?" grandma Peaches asked again, she was running out of patience. Angela wiped the trickle of tears rolling down her cheeks and calmed herself down.

"I'm sorry I scared you guys with my tears, it's nothing serious. I was just thinking of moving out, you know, getting my lease and becoming more independent."

Everyone could not believe what had just come out of Angela's mouth. That was the last thing they expected to hear from her. Grandma Peaches choked on her food and Tina grabbed a glass of water to offer her. "Wait, What, how, when…?" Ashley asked, still trying to process what she had just heard. "No way!" she did not even wait for a reply from Angela before concluding. "Your grandfather and father will never approve of this for Christ's sake. What has gotten over you?" Ashley began to scold Angela.

"Maybe the house is becoming too small for her." grandma Peaches suggested. "What do you want? More space? I noticed you have been buying tons of new clothes because of work so maybe your closet no longer contains them all. You can use any closet you want." but that was not her concern. Angela's phone began to ring. *Charles*, she pressed the power button to silent the phone. Once it finished ringing, Charles called again and again. "It's that boy right?" Ashley asked Angela.

"Isaiah?" she asked her mother, trying to play dumb.

"Oh, shut up, you pretender! You think your grandma and I don't know that you have been seeing someone else." Ashley dropped her spoon in annoyance and pushed her plate forward. "We were quiet because we did not want to intrude into your personal life but you want to overstep your boundary." Angela thought that she had been discreet enough; she did not know that her mother and grandma had been watching her closely. "You think you can keep it a secret, but you forgotten *that there is nothing hidden which cannot be manifested; neither was anything kept secret, but that it should come abroad (Mark 4 verse 22)* you cannot even introduce him to your family because he is not worth it."

"Mom!" Angela called her mother. "You are going too far."

Angela picked up her phone, stood up from the dining room table and stormed out of the house. The last words she heard before she left were *"do not be unequally yoked with unbelievers. For what partnership has righteousness with lawlessness? Or what fellowship has light with darkness? 2 Corinthian 6 verse 14."* When she left, everyone in the house became quiet, they did not expect that Angela will be the one to act in the way and manner that she just did. Right from her childhood, she had always done things right and in the way of the lord. What happened? What went wrong? "We need to pray" grandma Peaches

managed to say. She got up and Ashley followed her.

The three women walked into the sitting room and Tina was still shocked from what she just saw, her cousin began to open her mouth to raise a worship song unto God. When Angela got to where Charles was, she was moody. "What happened?" he asked her. She explained everything that had transpired between her and her family that evening. Charles comforted her and asked her to make sure she apologized to them when she got back home. "Your mom is right. I am currently married and so, you cannot introduce me to them just yet and even after I am divorce, won't I be stigmatized for being a divorcee with a child? Will they accept me?" he asked her these series of questions, "Because I have been thinking about these things too."

"Charles, just drive, when we get to that bridge, we will cross It," she said angrily. Why would Charles look down on himself in that way? While they drove, they talked about work and he told her how far he had gone in setting up his workspace. When she asked how he was able to source funds, he lied that he had requested a small loan for startups and his father had also supported him. He drove her to a small hotel far away from her neighborhood. "What are we doing here?" Angela asked him after he parked in front of the small building.

"Babe." he held her face and looked into her eyes. "Do you love me?" he asked, he had become serious.

"You know I do," Angela answered.

"Do you trust me?" he asked.

"Yes, you know I do," she answered impatiently. "Then stop asking questions and follow Me." they got out of the car and went into the hotel. He asked her to sit on one of the waiting chairs while he talked to the receptionist. He paid for a room and she handed him the key. When they got into the room, he began to kiss her impatiently and touch her inappropriately. "Oh baby, I love you so much," he said as his hands continued to travel up and down her body. Angela had gone out with Charles on different occasions, they had even gone to the club but the highest they have done was to kiss; French kiss but they have never been this close, in a confined space and she had never seen him in this mood before.

"Stop! What are you doing" she forced herself out of Charles's grip. "I want to make love to you, I want to feel your body closer to mine, I love you, Angela, let me show you how pleasant it feels." he let out a soft groan. "But I am not ready for this Charles; I promised my mother and grandmother that I will keep myself for my husband..."

"But I want to marry you remember?" Charles cut her off. "We are going to get married anyway" "But we are not." she insisted.

"There is never a right time or perfect time for a thing like this baby. Let me make love to you, let me make you feel something you have never felt before." he continued to convince her.

Angela realized that she was far away from home, it was late and there was no way she could fight her way out of this sticky situation she was in with Charles and so she gave in. They had slept off and completely lost track of time. When they woke up, it was morning already. They both checked their phones and saw tons of missed calls. Charles had missed calls from Stephanie, her parents and his dad, she had probably called everyone to ask if they knew about his whereabouts because he did not tell her that he was not going to go back home, he told her he wanted to go for a drive then left till the next morning. Angela also got missed calls from her family members and Isaiah. It was a Sunday morning and she had a solo to take during their choir ministration in church.

"Oh no!" she cried.

The house was empty when she got back home, she thought of dressing up and running to church immediately, "it is rather late than never." she thought but decided against it when she remembered what she had done the previous night.

She felt like she was too dirty to appear before God, she felt like filth. She went to her room, took a shower and lay on her bed, waiting for her family to come to scold her and thinking of the excuse she will give to Isaiah for not showing up in church. Only God knows what grandma Peaches and her mother will tell him when he asks them in church. The front door opened and she heard her mother's voice, grandma Peaches had probably said something funny because they were in a fit of laughter. Grandma Peaches always had a joke about each service. She really missed church. She heard a footstep walking down the hall and she quickly covered herself with a cloth and pretended to be asleep. Tina walked into the room and saw Angela sleeping.

"I know you are not sleeping Angela, stand up," she told her. Truthfully, she was not even sure if Angela was sleeping or not but she didn't want to disturb her. Angela quietly opened her eyes and looked at Tina. "Where did you go to last night? You got everyone worried."

"I went out with a friend," she answered.

"Isn't he the same person you hand a confrontation over yesterday?" Tina asked, Angela, did not reply nor gave any reaction. So Tina continued, "If you like him and you know that he is serious about you, bring him home and introduce him to everyone. Playing hide and seek will only harden their hearts and make them resent him more."

"It is not that easy," she answered and turned.

"Do you want to talk about it?" Tina offered a listening ear.

Angela shook her head. "It's ok if you are not ready to talk, but whenever you are ready, just know that I will be here."

"Thanks." Angela appreciated her effort. Tina had always been her favorite cousin. Her dad was Ashley's brother. He died when they were still teenagers and when her mother wanted to remarry; Tina opted to live with grandma Peaches but Tina had always been strong-willed, she loved God but she was not judgmental and it was hard to manipulate her unlike Angela and that was why they both have different views and ideas about life. "By the way, the verse of the day is Philippians 4:8. Open your bible and read it to my hearing."

Angela picked up her phone and opened the bible app then began to read, "Finally brethren, whatsoever things are true, whatsoever things are just, whatsoever things are pure, whatsoever things are lovely, whatsoever things are of good report; if there be any virtue, and if there be any praise, think on these things." she read and looked at Tina. "You need to apologize to Aunt Ashley and grandma Peaches. We are all family and it is not wrong of them to correct you when they think that you are erring. Grandma has forgiven you even before you will ask." Angela stood up from the bed and thanked Tina then she made her way downstairs while Tina changed her clothing's from her church outfit to a simple singlet top and palazzo pants. Grandma Peaches and Ashley were engrossed in their discussion about Angela when she walked in and they did not notice her presence.

"Try dialing her number again, maybe she will pick." grandma Peaches told Ashley. "Mom, if she wanted to, she will have. We called her so many times yesterday. Let's assume she was not with her phone, is it not proper for her to call us back when she saw the missed calls? I don't know what has gone wrong with Angela."

"Dial it one last time and if ..." "There's no need, I'm here already." Angela cuts her grandma off. "I am so sorry I did not take your calls last night, I had no idea my phone was ringing, I had put it on do not disturb mode when I was in church for choir practice yesterday and when I saw them this morning, I could not call back because I knew that you were in church. Ashley acted uninterested. Angela had never disrespected her nor her mother in that manner since she was born. This is because of that hoodlum that she was seeing. She even had the effrontery to sleep out. "Grandma, mom, I am deeply sorry for my actions last night, it was never my intention to act in that manner and I take full responsibility for it. Please forgive me." She wiped a tear. "Come baby" grandma Peaches called her close. "You have to be closer to God, you are drifting away. The

Angela I brought up would never act the way you acted" Angela hugged her grandma. Ashley sighed and walked out of the room. "You need to go talk to her," grandma Peaches told Angela. Angela walked to where her mother was. "Stop seeing him, he is bad for you," Ashley told Angela when she walked over to her.

"I know mama, but it's hard. I love him." Angela explained to her. "Angela, all my life, your grandmother, your father and I have tried our best to raise you in a good and godly manner. Where did we go wrong? Is Isaiah not a good man?" Ashley lamented. Angela started crying. They were quiet for a moment. Ashley realized that one can only force a horse to the stream but it cannot be forced to drink water. She will intercede for Angela through fasting and prayer. When Charles got home, he met Stephanie sitting on the couch. She was furious. "Hey baby." He greeted her and leaned in to give her a quick peck, she did not respond. "I'm sorry about last night. I did not know I would not come back and my phone was on silent all through," he explained. "You should have at least called. I was worried sick.

I'm pregnant Charles, you left your pregnant wife at home and alone and worried all through the night." she rolled her eyes.

Charles squatted in front of her and held her hands in his.

"You know the nature of my work..."

"...you were with another woman. You spent the night with Angela and I know."

Charles was taken aback by Stephanie's words. "I saw the text you sent to her before you left last night. Charles, what have I done to deserve this treatment?" Charles couldn't say a word. "I know we got married under circumstances beyond our control but haven't I tried to be a good wife? I dropped out of school to nurse our son, I try to love you the best way I can, to care for you and our son. I'm just scared that you will wake up one morning and leave me." She started to cry. "I'm not leaving you, babe, Angela is just a fling. You are the one in my house, not Angela," he told her to calm her down. He might not love Stephanie as much as he loved Angela but Stephanie is the mother of his son and his unborn child, he respected her a lot and did not want to offend her especially now that she was carrying his child. He stood up and held her to stand up to hug him. Can he leave her as much as he tells Angela? If he had his way, he will keep the two women but if he was asked to choose between the both of them, who will be the pick? He found himself in a dilemma.

CHAPTER THIRTEEN

THE SPIRIT OF CHRISTMAS

Christmas holiday was the most favorite holiday in grandma Peaches house, they would start shopping and decorating from the first week of December. Every two years, they will repaint the walls a rich creamy color and use red fur carpet around the house, the Christmas tree will be properly decorated with enough lightings. Everyone will take a family picture in front of the Christmas tree after the decoration, it was their tradition. Angela always made sure she slept in the sitting room till the next day morning after the decorations; she loved the feel and scent that the decorations came with. Her father and grandfather will be around for the holidays. Grandma Peaches would always say that the Christmas holiday brings the family closer together because the family tends to attend church together during Christmas. Isaiah invited Angela to his family house for dinner after the Christmas carol service in the church. Pastor Brown and Julie were very hospitable towards her, she enjoyed their company. Pastor Brown brought up the topic of Isaiah and Angela getting married soon and giving them beautiful grandchildren but Isaiah quickly died down the topic saying he did not want to rush Angela, he wanted them to take their time and be intentional about their union. At first, Angela was tensed. She knew Isaiah was not the only person she was dating. She was with him because it was what her grandmother wanted and because Isaiah seemed like a safer option. In her mind, if Charles disappointed her, she will fall back to him. Although she kept on seeing Charles, no one in the house-made mention of it to her ears, they all decided to pray and leave it all for God to handle. When she got back home, her grandfather had arrived. He came with lots of gifts for the whole house. Grandma Peaches made her husband's best soup and he ate it with glee, they were all excited as they talked about Angela's father arriving the next day. To lighten the moment, grandma Peaches suggested that they watch a movie about the nativity of Christ, for them to be reminded about the spirit of Christmas. It was not just a season to drink, eat and be merry, it is a time for sober reflection to be reminded of how our savior was born and why Christmas is a time for giving and showing love. Angela and Tina had planned to bake lots of cookies and take them to the nearest orphanage and spend time with the children. They also have a right to feel loved in this season.

CHAPTER FOURTEEN

DILEMMA

"Angela, do you have a tampon?" Tina whispered in her ears. "My period came early and I was thinking I will get some from the store tomorrow," she explained.

"Yes, come let's go upstairs." the two girls stood up and began to make their way out of the sitting room.

"Leaving so soon? The movie is not yet over." Ashley announced.

"We will be back" Angela announced as they left their sight.

While Tina was in Angela's bathroom using the tampon, Angela realized that she had not seen her period throughout the month.

She tried calculating manually and saw that it had been close to 40 days already.

She did not have any signs or symptoms of the period. When Tina finished, she came out of the bathroom, "let's go." "I want to pee, I will join you shortly." she lied then Tina left the room and went downstairs. Angela became discomforted. She dialed Charles's number, it rang the first two times and afterwards it went to voicemail. She was sad and angry at the same time. She went downstairs to join them. That night, she could not sleep; she kept on rolling from one side of the bed to the other. What if her fears became true? The next day morning before the whole family got up, Angela went to the nearest pharmacy to get a test strip, as she walked back home, the cold embraced her and Goosebumps grew on her skin, her fears intensified. Two red lines, Angela felt dizzy at once; she could not believe what she just saw. She was pregnant, by Charles, what was she going to do? She was not even sure how far she had gone and if people will begin to notice soon. She dialed Charles's number over and over again but still, it went to voicemail.

When her father arrived home, she was not as excited as she hoped to be because of the news. It had torn her apart. How will she explain to Isaiah, Pastor Brown, her family and the entire congregation that she was carrying the seed of another woman's husband? In the twinkle of an eye, all of her decisions flashed before her eyes.

"Are you ok?" Tina asked her. "You have been moody all morning."

"I'm fine, maybe I woke up on the wrong side of the bed." she lied.

"Escort me to the store; I'm going to get some toiletries. Maybe it will lighten your mood," she told Angela. Angela stood up and went out with her.

Later in the evening, Charles called her and asked her to come outside; he parked his car two streets away from theirs. She went out to see him. "All my calls kept going to voicemail," she told him as she entered the car.

"I'm sorry, Stephanie found out about us, we have to be more discreet," he explained.

"You are going to leave her anyway, so why are you being too careful around her?" she asked rudely but Charles did not say anything. She noticed his silence but did not pay any attention to it. There was a bigger fish to fry. "I'm pregnant." she broke the news.

Silence,

"Charles, you heard me, I said I am pregnant," she announced again.

"I heard you the first time, I am still trying to process what you just said," he said harshly. Angela was surprised because Charles was always soft-spoken towards her. "Do you want to keep it?" he asked her. "Is there an option?" she asked him. She thought when she told Charles about the pregnancy, he would be happy and see it as an excuse for them to finally be together but Charles was having none of it.

"It's a question," he stated. "Charles, this is our opportunity to finally be together, tell Stephanie I am pregnant by you, she will get mad and ask for a divorce," she suggested.

"I cannot." he closed his eyes and rested his head on his steering wheel. "I cannot put her under that stress, not right now."

"I do not understand," she said softly.

"Stephanie is also pregnant, she is in her second trimester," he said slowly.

The words rang in Angela's head over and over again. She did not even realize when tears began to flow from her eyes.

"so all these times you were busy badmouthing her to me, telling me you did not love her, sleeping with me and telling me that you loved me, you have been sleeping with her?" she asked furiously. "We live in the same house Angela, it's not that easy," he claimed.

"Oh my God, I have been such a fool! You have been lying to me and I trusted you blindly. You were just using me." she shouted. Her eyes had become red.

"I never lied to you Angela; everything I said was true…"

"Except when you said you will leave your wife for me," she said and left the car. She used the little time she had to walk back home to wipe her tears and prepare to be in a better mood. What will she do? Who will she run to? Her mother will say "I told you so," grandma Peaches will be so disappointed, her grandfather will claim that she misbehaved because she was over dotted on, she did not even want to think of what her father will say or do. She was the apple of his eyes, he was always happy to brag about her to his friends and his colleagues; it will break his heart. She could not sleep that night, she thought of a possible solution. What if she seduced Isaiah and he fell, she could lie that he was the father of her unborn child. What if the delivery time did not tally? When I get to that bridge, I will cross it. She texted Isaiah, "are you home?"

"Yeah, do you want to come by?" he replied to her.

"Yeah."

"Okay."

She quickly dressed up and informed her family members she was going to see Isaiah. When she got there, he was in his music room, creating beats and mastering music.

"You don't look happy," he said to her when he looked into her eyes. "You look like you are engulfed with sadness and you have been crying." "That's why I came here, for you to cheer me up." she smiled. "Come," he said as he tapped on the seat next to him signifying her to sit down. She did as she was told. He played the song he was listening to, "this is the song we wrote and recorded in the church." He informed her. They had written a song and performed it as a choir. Isaiah was mastering the song for production. "Let me take it to the part you came in." he quickly forwarded the song from his computer to where Angela's part started.

In him, we've found a friend

Someone who will always listen when we call

No matter the situation or circumstance

No matter where we have been or where we have gone Call on him and he will answer.

When her part was over, Isaiah pause the song and looked into her eyes. "You have such a beautiful voice, my dear, God really blessed you."

"Thank you." she blushed.

"I have listened to your part over and over again and each time, I thank God for bringing you into my life. You are a blessing and I cannot wait for the world to hear your voice. I am your biggest cheerleader." At this moment, guilt washed all over Angela. She should have taken Isaiah more serious, she shouldn't have given Charles all the love and attention she gave to him, and it should have been Isaiah. He had done nothing but love her genuinely even though she knew she was cheating on him. Sometimes, she would cancel on dates, other times, she will busy his call when she was with Charles then later give a lame excuse and he would still listen.

They never had a fight. As he was still talking, Angela leaned and gave him a kiss on the lips. It was their first kiss. Isaiah welcomed the warmth of her lips she began to deepen the kiss and wrapped her arms around his neck. Isaiah became still for a few seconds and withdrew from her. "This is a bad idea, we shouldn't go that far." he told her as he held her hands. "Get a grip of yourself," he said calmly without making her feel embarrassed for throwing her advances at him. "Maybe we should go out, eat pizza and ice cream then take a walk around town, we can talk about what is upsetting you." he offered but Angela refused.

"It's you I want." she moved close to him again, he shifted back. "Please Isaiah, do not reject me. I am yearning for you," she begged. She sounded desperate he thought to himself. "You have to go," he said firmly. He knew he was not a perfect person, while he was in college; he lived a reckless life until he encountered God for himself. His perspective about life changed and he made a vow to God to keep himself until he marries the woman that God had chosen for him. So when he told people about Jesus, he told them that he wasn't serving God because of the training his father had imbibed in him but because God has come through for him plenty of times when he thought all hope was lost. That was the issue Angela had, she grew up in a Christian home but she never really encountered God for herself, she just did whatever she was told was right and frowned away from what was wrong. She was the perfect daughter but that is one reason why she got easily swayed by the pressures of life. "You can't do this to me." Angela began to cry.

"I love you Angela" this was the first time he said it to her hearing, "and I know that it is not easy to get a grip of yourself at times like this but then, what will..."

"People say?" she cut him off.

"I do not care about what people will say when I know I am doing the right thing; I care about what God thinks. He watches us all."

"I'm in a mess," Angela said to herself when she realized that Isaiah was strong-willed and would not give in to her advances.

"What did you say?" he squint his eyes.

"Nothing, I need to go." she grabbed her purse.

"You said you are in a mess. What kind of mess have you gotten yourself into?" he stopped her from leaving. He begged the Holy Spirit to help him in dealing with her and to help her overcome what she was going through.

"Nothing," she repeated. "You are pregnant." He stated. Angela's eyes widened. How did he know? She thought. Then she quickly masked up her expression and said, "I do not know what you are talking about."

"Stop lying, your expressions already sold you out." he pressed more. "You wanted to seduce me and pin the pregnancy on me."

"Stop all these accusations, can I go now?"

Isaiah calmed himself down. "Stop lying to me, I already know. I deserve to know the whole truth and I promise you, in fact, I swear on my life that I will never tell a third party about the conversation we are about to have." he rubbed his head.

He could not believe what was happening right before his eyes. "Tell me the whole truth" he requested.

Angela sat down, she felt weak and defeated. She told Isaiah about everything that had happened between her and Charles and how she had been lying to him. By the time she was done talking, Isaiah was in tears. It took him some moments before he could utter a word. "If the God I serve can forgive me 7 times 70 times in a day, who is me not to forgive you?" he said quietly. Angela was surprised by his utterance. "It is hard, but I have to," he said amidst tears, "but we cannot continue to be in a relationship." more tears began to flow from her eyes; she knew it will be difficult for him to accept her and another man's child. She had played him and taken him for a fool all this while. He was even kind enough to forgive her.

"As I promised, I will not tell anyone about this conversation we just had, not even my father. we could just cook something up like we are not ready and do not want to waste each other's time but I strongly suggest that you inform your family about the baby before the bump begins to show so they don't get too surprised. I will never advise you for an abortion."

"Thank you." she appreciated his kind words.

"Angela" he called.

"Yeah," she answered with her croaked voice.

"The most important thing is to retrace your step back to God. Forget about everything that you have done, everything you are going through, he will forgive you and redeem you.

Remember the story of the lost son? Nothing can separate us from the love of the father." She nods her head. He held her hand and hugged her. "You will always be in my heart." He did not let her leave immediately because of the mood and situation she was in so he made her hot tea and offered her to drink. She fell asleep shortly after. In the evening, he drove her home.

CHAPTER FIFTEEN

A SAD CHRISTMAS

She decided to take Isaiah's advice and tell her family the truth. It was now or never, she thought, she did not want to sleep over it and change her mind or opt for an abortion, telling them will make it difficult for her to change her mind. After dinner, she told them that she had something to tell them, grandma Peaches and Ashley thought that Isaiah had finally proposed to her but the news she delivered was different. "Grandfather, Grandmother, Mom, Dad, Tina. You all have been family to me since day one and I cannot ask for a better choice of people to call my own." she choked on her words as she started crying again. Everyone knew the news they were expecting was not what they will get but they hoped that it was something their hearts could carry.

"Whatever I am about to say is not anyone's fault, you did not do any wrong in training me or teaching me the way of the lord, everything I have become is solely my fault and I take complete responsibility."

"What is going on my love?" Ashley asked.

"First of all, Isaiah and I are no longer in a relationship." She announced. Tina gasped. Did she finally choose the other guy over him? She thought to herself. "I am pregnant for someone else," she announced. Grandma Peaches collapsed. Every other thing that Angela had to say was not important at that point, everyone's main concern was getting grandma Peaches to the hospital. She was quickly rushed into the car and taken to the hospital. "If anything happens to my grandma, I will never forgive myself," Angela said out loud while pacing the hospital hallway. She was ashamed of herself, she did not even know how to walk to her family or make things right. Grandpa Miller was sitting in one of the waiting chairs while her dad was busy running around, trying to sort out the hospital requirements while Ashley called

Pastor Brown to inform him about grandma Peaches

condition to help in interceding on her behalf. Tina felt sorry for Angela; she could not imagine how she will be feeling or what going through her head at that very moment. She walked up to her and held her. "Be still, nothing will happen to grandma Peaches. She is just in shock." Tina comforted Angela. The doctor came out of the ICU and the entire family gathered around him. "She is stable now." He informed them. Angela let out a sigh of relief, "she is currently asleep and will be moved out of the ICU when she wakes up, then you can see her." "Thank you, Jesus", "Hallelujah", "God is good." Were the words that filled the air after the doctor's announcement. The next morning, grandma

Peaches was discharged from the hospital, Angela took it upon herself to prepare her meals, administer her medications and be on call whenever she needed assistance. She could not tell what was on grandma Peaches mind whenever she looked at her.

Was it disappointment?

Anger, or Pity? The entire family was unusually quiet to each other; it was like there was a thick cloud lingering in the air.

Tina was the only person who managed to act normal around Angela; she will engage her in discussions, surf through the internet together and made her laugh like nothing was happening. Angela was thankful for the presence of Tina in her life; she was the sweetest cousin she will ever ask for. It was a sad Christmas for everyone. For Christmas dinner, Ashley, Tina and Angela prepared the entire meal while Grandma Peaches was resting in her room. It was an uncomfortable moment for Angela because she noticed how her mother managed to avoid her in the kitchen. Tina, please pass me the meat stock, Tina come taste this and tell me what is lacking, and Tina help me get this or help me get that. She could not even get angry, she only felt sad and disappointed in herself for ruining her own life. Her mother did not even notice when she left the kitchen and went up to her room to cry like a baby. Maybe she did but did not care at that moment. During dinner, the aroma of the entire food nauseated Angela and she had to run to the nearest bathroom to vomit. "How can I go back to the table and face their staring eyes." She thought to herself. She stayed back for a few minutes before going back. She went back to the dining and saw that everyone had continued with their food as if nothing had happened. She sat down but refused to eat. "If the aroma can nauseate me like this, I wonder what will happen if I eat." She thought to herself. She was talking to herself most of the time except when she was around Tina because no one will talk to her even grandma Peaches who she is trying her best to care for. "Grandma Peaches and Grandma Miller," Tina called. "The both of you are the head of this family and should please address this issue today, I mean tonight. I do not like this atmosphere. Good or bad, Angela is still a part of our family. Yes, she has made a mistake but nonetheless, she is one of the sweetest persons I have encountered in my whole life." Tina paused, she was tired of the way everyone was handling the issue. "Most single people have sex every day, some get lucky and get away with it, some get pregnant and opt for an abortion, only a few just like Angela agree to keep the baby because two wrongs cannot make a right. Merry Christmas!"

"Do you know the disgrace she has brought upon herself and this family?" Ashley replied. "Remember when she came back here after graduating from college, how members of the church came to visit with gifts because they saw her as a special child. Do you know how I raise my shoulders high because Angela is my daughter and because she has never been caught in a compromising position before?" as she continued, her pitch became higher. "She is a member of the church choir, she dated the pastor's son," tears were beginning to flow from her eyes, "do you know how many times pastor Brown joked with me about becoming in-laws?" She turned to face Angela with tears in her eyes. "Now she has gone and got herself pregnant for someone we do not even know in the family, she is carrying a bastard in her womb!" Ashley shouted. Angela began to cry too. The words her mother said were hurtful but she was happy that Ashley was beginning to voice out her opinion since the announcement of her pregnancy. Healing will start from here.

"Ashley!" Grandma Peaches called her. "Stop, these words of yours will not change anything that has happened; you are only opening more wounds." After dinner, Grandpa Miller called the whole family together to address the issue. "According to Tina, what has happened, has happened. We cannot go back in time but our response to this will determine whether things will get better or not." He paused, took a sip of water and called his granddaughter's name, "Angela."

"Yes Grandpa" she replied to him.

"We need to meet the father of your child, have you even informed him yet?" He asked her. "Not yet, but I will, I just wanted my family to find out first." She lied. How will she explain to them that she had told Charles and he was opting for an abortion?

When she got into her room, she began to dial Charles's number but unfortunately, her calls kept on going to voicemail.

"Have you reached him?" Tina would ask every fifteen minutes. Angela would reply by just shaking her head. For two weeks straight, she heard nothing from Charles, not even his random messages when he was not available.

CHAPTER SIXTEEN

EVERYONE KNOWS

Angela walked into her room and found Tina sitting on her bed reading her bible. It seemed like their lifestyles had switched. Tina was always the wild one who had a different opinion about everything and Angela was the quiet and obedient one who wanted to do everything right and pleases everyone. If grandma Peaches believed in voodoo, she would have thought that someone had cast an evil spell on Angela.

"Right now?" Tina paused to ask.

"Yeah."

"Ok." She used dog ears to mark the page she was on and placed the bible down. "I am listening."

"I am so sorry for your loss." Angela sympathized with her Tina was commemorating her father's death anniversary. Earlier in the day, she had visited her father's graveside. Her eyes were in tears. They sat in silence for about ten minutes, Angela understood that Tina needed her privacy; she needed time alone to calm down and console herself so she patted her on her back and left the room. Michelle came to the house immediately Angela sent her a text to tell her that they needed to talk and it was very important. When Michelle previously told Angela about Charles, she had asked for them to see so she could explain things to her but Angela never showed up even some times when she brought it up, Angela will brush off the issue like she was not interested and Michelle assumed that Angela had forgotten about Charles and let go. Little did she know that Angela had secretly been seeing Charles, and had even been sleeping with him. "I blame myself for everything that has happened" Michelle cried when Angela told her the whole situation.

"Why?" She asked her. "Were you the one who made me date him?"

"I was the one who told you to go ahead and date people" she answered.

"You did not tell me to date a married man, besides, you warned me about Charles when I told you about him. I just did not know what came over me." Tears rolled down her cheeks.

"I know where he lives," Michelle stated. "How can he get you pregnant and disappear into thin air?"

Angela became ashamed of herself once again, she had been dating Charles for months but she did not know where he lived or anyone from his family to contact.

What had she done to herself? Angela got up and began to dress up, she informed Tina who also volunteered to go with them. The three ladies got into Michelle's car and she drove off. Charles's house was just eight minutes away from Angela's neighborhood. It was a small house with a big courtyard.

Michelle pulled over in the driveway and the three women came down, she led the three of them to the front door and knocked. It took a while before someone opened the door.

"Hi," a beautiful young girl in her teens greeted them.

"Hello Dear, I'm looking for Stephanie, is she home?" Michelle spoke softly to her.

"Stephhhhh....." The girl called. "They are here for you." "Ok" Stephanie answered from inside the house.

"She will be with you shortly" the girl stated, and locked the door again. Angela was so anxious, she was about to stand face to face with the woman she had heard so much about from her husband. She did not even know how she looked and she never bothered before now, all she cared about was that Stephanie was the one blocking her way from being with the love of her life. "Good evening" Stephanie greeted as she opened the door.

"Michelle, Hi" she acknowledged her when she spotted her.

Stephanie was beautiful in her way, she was pregnant but she still retained her shape, with no excess fat around her body. She had plump lips and long straight legs. Angela felt inferior standing in front of Stephanie. "No wonder he is having a hard time letting her go," she thought. "Will Charles ever belong to me?"

"Hello Stephanie" Michelle smiled. "This is my friend Angela" she pointed at Angela and Stephanie directed her eyes towards her, Angela was looking so calm and innocent in her black flare gown that ended just below her knee. Her eyes were red from tears and they looked swollen. "And this is her cousin Tina." "We are here to see Charles." Michelle requested.

"He is not in," Stephanie stated. She had known Michelle from their high school days; she had joined the school Michelle and Charles had attended. They were not friends but there were classmates and were cordial with their selves. "This is important Stephanie." Michelle pleaded with her eyes.

"Why is she here?" Stephanie asked Michelle, directing her gaze to Angela. Angela remembered when Charles had told her that Stephanie had found out about them and he wanted to be more discreet. "Look Stephanie, I know you already found out about Charles and me but for God's sake, if he is in let us know, it is really important."

"As I said, Charles is not in. He is not even in town, he travelled. I am not a liar" she eyed Angela. "Is there any way we can reach him?" Michelle asked.

"He specifically told me not to give the contact with which I can reach him to anyone, I mean anyone." She answered. Everyone understood the hidden meaning behind her last words. "But if the information you want to pass is that important, I am his wife, you can tell me, I will relay the information to him when we talk." "Well, tell that lying and cheating husband of yours that his girlfriend is pregnant and he has to show his face and take responsibility, he does not have the right to leave town or cut communication with her after she told him about her condition." Tina blurted. She did not understand why Michelle and Angela were so soft-spoken towards Stephanie when she was being a brat, rubbing in the fact that she knows about Angela's and Charles's escapades. Instead of her chastising her husband who could not keep his manhood between his legs, she is here trying her best to bring Angela down.

Stephanie was first taken aback by Tina's revelation and how blunt she was. *So Charles had gotten her pregnant.* She thought to herself. "Alright, will you leave my house now?" She told them holding her stomach. "Yes, nothing is amusing here anyway," Tina said first then walked away, Angela followed but Michelle stayed back to talk to Stephanie for a few minutes.

"I explained to her that Angela never knew that Charles was married from the onset and that she found out along the way, even when she wanted to leave, Charles persuaded her to stay. I made her understand that her husband also had a hand to play in this whole mess." Michelle told them when they were inside the car driving back to the house.

"There is no use crying over spilled milk, what we want to hear is her husband's whereabouts," Tina replied. "She does not know, he left town urgently and they only talk on the phone when he calls her," Michelle answered her. "That was the only useful information I got from her." Angela was quiet all through the ride home. If she was so important to Charles, he would have reached out to her just as he was reaching out to his family, she thought. When Angela got home, she sat down on her bed and began to cry, streaks of tears falling from her eyes one after the other. She turned and saw her bible, "It has been a long time" she thought to herself. "Does God still remember my name?", Does he still love me?", If I pray, will he still answer?" She asked herself these questions. "Well, I won't know if I don't try." She said to herself and picked up the bible.

She opened a random page and the first words that she set her eyes on were, *"for I am persuaded, that neither death, nor life, nor angels, nor principalities, nor powers, nor things present, nor things to come, nor height, nor depth, nor any other creature, shall be able to separate us from the love of God, which is in Christ Jesus our Lord* (Romans 8 verses 38 and 39)." She knelt and began to thank God for his undying love and for sending his Son to bring salvation to mankind. She prayed for a while and told God that she wanted to feel his presence in her life once again and that she will let go of the past for a fresh beginning. As she prayed, she felt Goosebumps crept onto her skin; she felt shivers from the Holy Spirit. She realized that it had been a while she felt connected to God even though she barely missed church she didn't feel as she was feeling as she prayed. Grandma Peaches walked into her room to talk to her but found Angela kneeling beside her bed completely lost in prayer, she smiled and walked out of the room. The following week, Angela went to the hospital nearest to her workstation to register for antenatal care, she met a member of St. John's Baptist church who had also registered in that hospital. Angela knew that the moment the woman would leave the hospital; she will go ahead to spread the news like it was the gospel but she had mentally prepared her mind for it, besides it was her fault and she was willing to shoulder the responsibilities. After church, Pastor Brown summoned Angela to his office, "what is this that I am hearing?" "It's true sir," Angel answered him.

Pastor Brown looked down and shook his head in disappointment. "I expected more from you, my dear." A trickle of tears dropped from Angela's eyes, "I expected more from myself too. I am so sorry I let you and everyone who believed in me down." She apologized.

"I will have to suspend you from singing in the church choir and partaking in other workers activities until your baby is born." He told her.

"Yes sir." She answered calmly.

"It hurts me to do this, but it is the doctrine of the church, you are not the first to be in such a situation so do not look down on yourself, you not serving in the church do not mean that you cannot have a personal relationship with him. I will be here for you just in case you need counselling or prayers."

"Thank you, Pastor, to be sincere, I did not expect such kind words from you, I expected it to be scolding all the way, Thank you." She appreciated him.

"Wipe your tears," he handed her a tissue "Jesus loves you."

She stood up from the Visitor's chair and left his office.

When she got out of the office, she saw Isaiah standing in the hallway, talking to a girl from the choir, they were chatting happily, and maybe she was exaggerating in her mind because she was jealous. She turned to follow the opposite route. "Angela!" Isaiah called as he sighted her. She turned and the other girl was no longer in sight. "I was waiting for you." He told her. Angela wanted to reply but she knew that her voice will betray her because all she did for the past days was cry and she did not want him to know that. She nodded her head in response to what Isaiah had said. "I know you have been having a hard time in church, I have been hearing stuff and I know you have too, sometimes I wonder where they got their version of the story from" he chuckled to lighten the air before

he continued, "do not take those words to heart, it is only normal for humans to respond to situations like this." Angela nods in response. "Most of the people talking have skeletons in their closet too, but then they feel that they have the right to judge just because theirs is not in the open."

When Angela was able to compose herself, she responded to Isaiah, "Thank you." She smiled. "How are your health and that of the baby?" he asked her.

"We are both fine." She smiled again. He did not bother to ask her if she was still crying over what had happened because it was obvious, her eyes were swollen and she had developed dark circles.

"Alright then." He tapped her shoulders and left her.

CHAPTER SEVENTEEN

SAD NEWS

One fateful night, while Angela was studying her bible, her phone rang. It was her quiet time with God, she picked up the phone to silent it. Charles, he was the caller. She had not seen his call on her phone for over a month. She quickly kept her bible and picked the call. "I'm parked at our usual spot, please come out." Then he ended the call. Angela quickly jumped down from the bed and wore a big gown over the singlet and shorts she was wearing, she wanted to ask Tina to accompany her but thought against it, she did not want to scare Charles away, Tina had come home angry, she had an altercation with a church member on the street because of

Angela besides, she wanted to talk to him and know why he was out of town, what had happened. If she needed answers, she will have to go alone.

Tina was walking back home peacefully on the street, when she got to a bending corner she noticed three women pointing fingers at her, she did not look at them properly as she was trying to mind her business, but the moment she walked past they began to laugh. Tina turned back to look to see who they were and what had warranted that stupid behavior so she went to them. "Excuse me, have we met somewhere before?" she had asked them. She recognized two out of the three. The first one answered and said, "Aren't you the cousin to that pretender, the pregnant virgin." They all laughed again. Tina's anger went from zero to a hundred percent in a split second. She did not want to be violent by starting a fight, she was outnumbered so she decided to use her most powerful tool; her mouth. "Oh wait! I recognize you now. You are Christy right?" she asked pointing a finger at her face. "Does that change the fact that your cousin could not even produce the father of her unborn child?" the woman replied sarcastically. "At least she is doing something honorable, she is keeping the baby." Tina clapped back. "But a little bird told me they saw you hold your teenage daughter's hand into an abortion clinic. How old is she? 16, 17?" Tina smirked. The woman kept quiet. "Oh yeah, it was a secret until just now that I have revealed it to your friends" Tina knew those women had loose mouths and the entire church would find out about it. "Is your deacon husband also aware of this? Is Pastor Brown aware? Sure God will be aware, you can't fool that Man" Tina asked her. The woman looked down. "As for you, God will judge you," Tina said pointing to the other woman she could recognize. "You made everyone believe Sister Rita was a liar when she came out to say Elder Moses abused her. You silenced a victim just because you wanted to protect your brother's image." Tina said. "But have you ever heard me spreading it to the world? Everyone has a secret that they are not proud of but you chose to shame others for theirs that got revealed." She turned to go her way, after taking about

five steps she turned back and said, "God be with you all." She smirked and continued her journey back home.

She never knew that the constant inflow of gossips that arrive at her table would help her to defend someone she cares about someday. She felt bad for rubbing their issues to their face but they should have minded their business and not mess with her for no reason. She was angry when she got home and narrated the event to grandma Peaches, Ashley and Angela.

"Hey." He greeted her when she got into the car. "Hey." She replied him "I'm sorry I did not reach out to you." He apologized. "Did your wife tell you I was at your place?" she questioned him. "Yes she did, when I was away." He answered her. The atmosphere was awkward for them both because they had not talked for a long time and there was a lot of things yet to be said but there was no time. "I told you I was pregnant and you disappeared into thin air."

"I know you have been through a lot and what I did was unacceptable but I had to run, some guys are after me." He told her.

"I have been out of town, some guys are after me," he explained. "After you? Why?" she asked.

"Long story." he waved the issue off. "How are you and the baby?" he asked her.

"You are the father of my unborn child and if you love me as much as you claim to, then I deserve the right to know." She knew what he was trying to do but she was having none of it, she needed answers to all her questions.

"Look, I know I haven't told you this before, but I have been shipping stuff," he said in a very hushed tone.

"Stuff like what?" she demanded to know, she was not going to back down. "Drugs" he sounded almost inaudible. Angela's eyes grew wide, she never even suspected it. Charles had told her he was working on setting up a small office which he never did. Angela did not bother to ask him about his source of income, or where he got all the money he used to take care of his family and spent on her. "When I came back from college, I helped put an old friend; Ricky. I gave him some contacts to work with, after gaining their trust, he dumped them, sold their products and ran away with the money and they came for me. I had to run out of town, I snuck in this night to see my family and you. I will be leaving at dawn." She had prepared herself a thousand times for the excuse that Charles will give when he comes back into her life but she never knew that his reasons will be more than what she thought they will be. Oh, Charles! Angela was in denial; she did not want to believe her man was a drug dealer. "So, tell me, how far you have gone?" he asked her and took her hands. She realized he did not want to talk about the issue more than he had already done and she decided to let the sleeping dog lie. "I have registered for antenatal; the baby is doing just fine. I will be three months in five days." They talked for a while and Charles told her he needed to leave as it was getting darker. When Charles left, he made sure to call Angela to check up on her and the baby. On one of their conversations, she made it clear to him that she did not want to continue a romantic

relationship with him even though it was hard for her because she already fell for him completely but the only relationship they could have was a relationship as co-parents because she had promised God that she did not want to go back to the pit where she was coming from.

Charles accepted because it was an over-the-phone conversation and he did not want to pester her too much, he thought that once he gets back he will lure her back; physical presence is more powerful. Angela got home from work one evening, her baby bump was beginning to show slightly, she and Tina had planned to visit the mall to get some few things, she wanted to start buying her thins little by little, Charles also supported her by sending her some money. During their last conversation, he had told her that Stephanie had given birth to a boy. She was in the kitchen helping her mother with dinner when her phone rang.

"Am I speaking to Miss Angela?" the caller asked.

"Yes, who am I unto?"

"I am Officer Murray" Angela's demeanor changed. Why will a policeman be calling her by this time of the day? Did it have anything to do with Charles? Just like he was reading her thoughts, he continued; "Charles Wood had been shot dead a few minutes ago and your number was the last he dialed on his phone. It was saved with the name "My Angel" we are trying to reach out to his family members to inform them of what has happened before further investigations." The officer kept on talking but Angela had zoned out. "Hello, ma'am, are you there?" he asked but she could no longer hear him. She fell flat and collapsed. By the time she woke up, she was lying down on a hospital bed.

An oxygen mask was worn on her nose with cannula was inserted in it. Tina was sitting next to her bed. When Tina noticed Angela had gained consciousness, she alerted the nurses. They came, checked her vital and told Tina that Angela was stable. Angela remembered the last conversation she had on the phone before she lost her consciousness and tears flowed down from her eyes. "Tell me it was a dream." She said calmly. Tina could not bear to see her cousin in such a state, she held herself from crying too. When she woke up at the hospital, she was told that she had lost her baby. The next day, she got discharged and was taken home. She went back to Charles's house to visit Stephanie. She apologized for everything that had happened. There was no use holding a grudge for one another, because she had lost the baby and her relationship with Charles was over. Stephany and Angela decided to let bygones be bygones.

CHAPTER EIGHTEEN

ROAD TO REDEMPTION

Ashley suggested for Angela to leave town and go back to her father for some time, maybe changing her environment will help in her healing process. The people around here no longer look at her with that eye of admiration that they use to and it will be difficult for her to adapt.

"But I have a job here." Angela objected.

"Your job is nothing compared to your mental health. You are not going to be with your father forever, just long enough for you to be better." Ashley persisted. She felt sorry for her daughter, for everything she had gone through in the past few months, in a way, she blamed herself for how Angela had turned out. At first, she was angry with her daughter but when she sat down to think about it, she knew she had put too much pressure on Angela right from when she was a baby. Everything was imposed on her, do this, don't do this, stay focused and all, they were good advice but she should have let her live a little at least she wouldn't have fallen for Charles; he was her first love and it was difficult for her to let go.

Angela quit her job, her boss was sad to let her go; she was a fast learner and had become an important member on staff with the company. He gave her a recommendation letter and prayed for her to excel wherever she planted her feet. "I am sure there will always be an opening for you whenever you chose to relocate back here. I will call you from time to time."

He told her. Angela went into her office and cleared her desk. Her colleagues only knew what was happening when she was dropping her office keys at Beatrice's table. There was a group hug and she promised to visit them whenever she was in town. Since the turn of events, the relationship between grandma Peaches and Angela had been strained. Angela knew that she hurt grandma Peaches badly and if she had a choice, she would stay back to mend whatever had been broken. Angela got to grandma Peaches room and knocked on the door. "Come on in," she called. She had no idea who was knocking on the door but she knew that it had to be a member of her family.

"Grandma," Angela called when she walked in, she stood in front of the bed grandma Peaches was lying on.

"Hi Angela, come here." She waved her over, "Sit down." Angela did as she was told and grandma Peaches sat up.

"I have packed my things, I'm leaving tomorrow." She told grandma. Grandma Peaches heaved a sigh, "Grandma, I am sorry for disappointing you and putting you through so much emotional stress. I promise you that I have learnt my lesson and I am still learning and when I come back here, I will be better physically, spiritually and emotionally. I love you so much."

"I love you too my dear granddaughter. I am praying for you, I will miss your presence around here but this is what is best for you." She opened her arms and Angela embraced her. "Remember to see Pastor Brown tomorrow before you leave."

"Ok, grandma." She looked into grandma Peaches eyes and saw that her eyes were red. She stood up from the bed and went into her room.

Tina was sitting on the bed, next to her arranged box. "I'm bad at saying goodbyes," Tina said before Angela could say a word. They were cousins, they did not always have the same opinion about things but they loved each other so much. Angela always appreciated the fact that Tina had her back no matter what whether good or bad. "So I came here now because you might not see me tomorrow morning."

"We will always talk on the phone, do video chats, I will also visit from time to time," Angela said. "Oh come on! You know it is not the same thing."

Tina argued.

"I know," Angela replied feeling defeated. "But it is better than not communicating at all." Angela covered the box on the bed and zipped it. "Come here." She called Tina and pulled her in for a tight hug. "Spend the night in my room." Angela requested. "I do not want to sleep alone."

"Ok, I will."

"Thanks."

"Have you told Isaiah you are leaving?" Tina inquired.

"No, is there any need?" Angela asked.

"It isn't necessary though, but I think he deserves to know because he has been a good friend to you all this while."

"I am going to Pastor's Brown's house in the morning; I stop by at his place on my way back."

"Good."

The two ladies talked to their selves until it was very late and they had to retire for the night.

The next morning as early as 6 am, Angela woke up from her sleep, and was alone in bed. Tina had left her; she had told her that she might not see her but she thought that sleeping in the same room with her would and least make things different. Tina did not like losing people that is why she barely got attached to people. She had friends, yes, but she always built a wall up to prevent from getting too attached. She had a breakdown when she lost her father and her relationship of three years broke off almost immediately after, he cheated. In his defense, she completely shut everyone off even when he wanted to be there for her. What happened with the other lady was just physical but Tina knew it was more than her shutting everyone off. he had been cheating but she just had to find out, she refused to look past it and broke off the relationship.

Angela freshened up and quickly drove to Pastor Brown's house. She joined them for breakfast and he prayed with her afterwards. "Call me when you need anything. I am always available." He told her as he and his wife saw her off to the driveway. "Sir, I appreciate your love and care towards me even when the rest of the world turned their back on me. You are indeed a man of God and a father and I pray that God continues to bless you and strengthen you and your family." Angela prayed.

"Amen!" Pastor Brown and his wife Julie chorused.

Isabelle came out of the house holding a small box. "I made these for you." She smiled. "Thank you," Angela replied smiling, she was unsure of what was in the box though. Angela and Isabelle bonded when she was still together with Isaiah and Isabelle were one of the few people who did not judge her by her mistakes.

"Cookies, that's what is in the box" she answered the unasked question.

"I will eat this with fresh juice while I am on the train. Thanks."

She thanked her.

Isabelle leaned close to her and spoke in her ears, "Have you seen my brother?"

"Nope. I will stop by his place on my way home." She whispered in Isabelle's ears.

"Ok" she answered out loud.

"Ok sir, ok ma, I have to go now." She got into her car and drove off.

When she got to Isaiah's apartment, she knocked. It took some time for him to open the door.

"Hey, Angela." He greeted her when he saw her, "I was not expecting you, and sorry I took so long to reply, I was saying my morning prayers."

"Good morning." She greeted him.

"Come inside." He offered.

"Thanks." She smiled and went inside the house.

"To what do I owe this morning visit?" he asked. Before she could reply, he asked another question, "What can I offer you?" "I ate at your parent's house…"

"Oh," he mouthed raising his brows. He became more curious to know what Angela had come to tell him.

"I'm leaving."

He looked confused, "Leave to where?" he asked.

"I am leaving town indefinitely. My mom suggested, not a

suggestion, she insisted I leave for a while, to get myself together. Everything is messed up." She told him. How she managed to be free with Isaiah after everything that had happened between them was still a surprise to her.

"When are you leaving?" he asked her. He looked sad.

"This afternoon. I've got my bags packed, my train ticket booked," she smiled "All I have to do right now is to go home, dress up, look pretty, then be on my way." She laughed. Isaiah could feel the sadness behind her words.

"You could have just told her that you didn't want to go if you do not want to," Isaiah told her. "Stop letting everyone dictate their idea of you to you. You are a whole human being and you have to start living." He told her.

"I know" her eyes began to gather tears. In the past few months, she had cried more than she smiled and every time, she wonders how come there are still tears available to come out.

"But for now, this is what is best. I need it."

"Ok. If it is what is good for you."

"Alright, I stopped by to tell you." She stood up, he stood up after her.

"God still loves you despite all that you have been through. Do not let anyone make you feel like you do not deserve grace because you made a mistake." He said to her.

"Yes," she nodded.

"Remember he left the 99 for just one. Tell them how special you are because Jesus went after you."

"Thank you." She continued to nod. "I will reach out."

"You better do."

He walked her to her car and she went back home. Tina was still not back, but Michelle had arrived to spend her last moment with her before she left.

When it was time, grandma Peaches hugged her tightly. "Come soon my grandchild." She planted a kiss on her cheeks. Ashley and Michelle drove Angela to the train station to see her off and grandma Peaches walked back inside the house.

Grandma Peaches phone rang. "Hello, who is it?" she asked as she answered the phone. "It's me, Tina. Has she left?" she asked. "You've missed her, huh, Ashley and Michelle just saw her off to the train station. If you hurry up, you could see her before she leaves." Grandma Peaches advised.

"If I wanted to say goodbye, I would have called her phone instead. I just wanted to confirm so that I can come back home and have my beauty sleep." Tina always tried to use humor to cover her pain. Grandma Peaches ended the call without saying a word.

Angela was moving to another city, the city where her dad

works to start life afresh, to heal from all the pains and heartache this

small town had given her. Maybe she will get better someday, maybe

she will meet someone new and fall in love, maybe one day she will

forget but it will never come until she takes the step of redemption.

CHAPTER NINETEEN

HEALING AWAITS

The breeze of a new city welcomed Angela; she struggled to bring down her two boxes and handbag from the train. People were struggling to come down. Her father had promised to pick her up from the train station. She went to a corner to settle before bringing out her phone to dial her father's number.

"Hello dear, have you arrived?" he asked her when he picked up the call.

"I just got here daddy." She told him.

"Hold on dear, I just left the office, I will be with you shortly."

"Ok." She ended the call.

She waited for a few minutes then her phone rang again.

"Hello, daddy."

"Where are you? I'm at the station."

Angela described where she was to her father, "ok, I'm coming your way."

She got up from the chair she was sitting in, she wanted to buy a bottle of water quickly before her father would get to her, as she stood up, a guy rushed past her and knocked down her big box on the floor. "Sorry," he said and turned to help.

"Are you blind?" she said almost immediately. She was not a rude person but maybe the stress she was going through brought out that side of her. When he heard what she said, he walked away and left her to struggle with her big box alone.

She bought the water before her father got to where she was. He hugged her tightly and helped her with her big box; she carried the small box and her handbag and followed him to where he had parked his car.

"Hey Richard, meet my daughter Angela." Her father introduced her to a young man leaning on his car. He was the same guy who had bumped into her earlier.

They looked into each other's eyes without saying a word. "Dad, I am tired, can we go now?" she said and opened the back seat and entered the car.

"Wait, have you guys met before?" Spencer asked Richard, he was confused.

"Long story." He answered and helped Spencer carry the box to put into the car trunk. They both got into the car.

"How was your journey honey?" he asked Angela.

"Long. I just want to sleep." She answered him dryly. "Your mom said you have been doing a lot of that lately."

"It's a phase, it will pass." She answered him.

Richard sat down quietly listening to their conversation, he didn't know that the person he had bumped into earlier was his boss's daughter who they had come to pick up at the station, he felt stupid for being petty. Richard assisted Spencer to bring the things down and roll them to the front door.

They got into the house, Angela slouched on the couch. Everything exhausted her.

"You might want to go inside and sleep, your room is the second door by your left. I had the housekeeper prepare it for you." Spencer had moved into a bigger apartment since the last time Angela was there.

"Thank you." She stood up and began to walk towards her room. Richard offered to help her with her boxes. When he entered the room, he quickly used the opportunity to apologize. "Hum Angela," he scratched the back of his head. "I'm sorry for what happened earlier, I was in a rush to get back to my boss before he came back with his daughter so he wouldn't have to wait for me, but unfortunately I bumped into you. I should have helped you pick up the bag when I fell but I didn't and I accept I am wrong."

"Next time, when you are in a glasshouse, don't throw stones. Excuse me." Was Angela's reply.

"She is impossible," Richard thought to himself and left the room.

"Richard, can you please get the papers from the car?" Spencer tossed the car keys to him. "I will be at the study."

"Alright."

Angela laid down on the bed in her room, she felt sleepy on her way there but sleep seemed to have vanished when her back touched the bed. Maybe it was because she had a lot on her mind, maybe it was because her body had not adapted to the environment she was in. She recounted all her experiences since she arrived in town. Angela didn't know why she was rude to Richard even when he came to apologize. She was not a rude person neither did she intend to become one. She made a mental note to apologize for her bad behavior the next time they crossed paths and blame it on tiredness.

She thought of everything and everyone she had left behind, her grandma, her mother, her sweet cousin, her best friend Michelle and Isaiah of course. Thinking about it, she needed to take a break to heal. She thought about Charles, "In blessed memory" she whispered to herself. Although she never talked about it after Charles was buried but she missed him dearly, her hands subconsciously travelled to her stomach and she remembered *the baby*. Trickles of tears began to escape her eyes. She stayed in the room for a while until she fell asleep.

A loud noise woke her up from her sleep; it was the sound of shattered glass. She jumped down from the bed and rushed out.

"Dad are you ok?" she asked. When she got to the dining, she saw Richard trying to sweep the debris. "You are still here?" she asked him but he didn't answer her. "I heard a loud noise, are you ok?" Spencer asked when he got to where they were standing.

"I'm sorry sir, it slipped when I was trying to place it back in its cupboard after drinking water." He explained.

"It's nothing, as long as you have no cut on you," Spencer answered.

"Ï have to go now, I will see you at the office tomorrow." He said goodbye to his boss.

Angela followed him to the door and apologized for her behavior, she blamed it on stress just as she had planned and he accepted.

"Let me microwave something for us to eat," Spencer told his daughter.

"I am not hungry, I want to go back to sleep." She sounded bored.

"That is all you have done since you came here, will you at least sit down and have a conversation with your father?"

She felt defeated and decided to sit down and have a chat. Maybe it will help because going back to that room means only one thing, *"Thoughts & Tears."*

"I do not like the way you are looking now Angela, I know you have been through a lot but you have to brighten up. It's so obvious that you have been crying your eyes out."

"I cannot help it, daddy, everything just keeps coming back in my head. I have failed everyone who believed in me, I lost my baby and the love of my life. It is not that easy." She explained.

"I know." He rubbed her shoulders. "At a point in everyone's life, they have all committed grave mistakes; I'm not excluded. But when things go south, we have to pick up the pieces and keep pushing. We cannot continue to beat ourselves up when

Jesus no longer see us that way. There is no condemnation."

"Daddy." Tears began to flow down her cheeks.

"Stop crying, I do not want you to get sick on my watch." He stood up and hugged her then patted her hair.

"Can you tell me one mistake you have made in your life?" she wanted him to share with her, maybe his healing process will help her.

"I am not supposed to say this to you, but you are no longer a kid so you can handle it," he told her, she shook her head. "I cheated on your mom once and I got caught." He rubbed his beard. It took him enough courage to admit to his daughter that he had been unfaithful.

"Oh my God, when did this happen?" her eyes grew open.

"Two years ago." He answered quietly.

"How come I am just hearing about it." she asked.

"It was because we chose not to tell you, that was not the side of life we wanted to project to you as our child. We wanted you to grow with the idea of a perfect family where peace and love abounds." He regretted not saying the truth to her sooner, maybe, just maybe if she had known, she will have understood the consequences of being with a married man and how it can destroy a family, and maybe she will have refrained.

"How did mom take it?" she asked him. She was shocked by the revelation; she had never heard it from either of her parents.

Maybe it was her fault, she had her parents but was disconnected from them most of the time, she was lost in the love that her grandma had shown to her that she never really enjoyed staying with her parents despite the fact that she loved them dearly. "She said she forgave me but I know she hasn't, it's hard, or maybe she has, but then I felt like she is having a hard time forgetting the whole scenario. What do you think she is doing at her mother's place?" he asked her.

"Oh, I never really thought of it that way." She never asked. "I just assumed that it was some sort of arrangement between the both of you and maybe she hated here as much as I did." Spencer smiled.

"Why did you do it?" she asked him.

"Do we have a reason for all our actions?" he asked her back.

She thought about it and gave no reply because he was right. "It was just a moment of weakness, I gave in to it and it has ruined my marriage." He stood up and took a glass to fetch water. "Is she asking for a divorce?" Angela asked. She felt guilty; she needed to establish a better relationship with both her parents.

"No, she said she will come back when she heals from her pain. We talk every day though and I was around last Christmas, but she is getting too comfortable without me and it scares me." He revealed his fear.

"Did you love this other lady?"

"No, I haven't loved any other woman aside from your mom since we have been together. It was a moment of weakness like I said. It was just physical but it did not justify my actions." "Hmm..." she remembered when Isaiah told her everyone had a skeleton in their closet and nobody's life was perfect she never knew her parents were included.

She saw that she was beginning to experience life for what it truly was; she was seeing life beyond the façade it was clothed with. "God will help us all." She managed to say.

"I have called your mom to inform her that you have arrived, I know you forgot to do that. I told her you were so tired when you arrive so you went to sleep immediately. You can call her in the morning."

"Thanks, dad."

They prayed together and retired for the night.

Grandma Peaches had missed her granddaughter so much, everyone knew that a lot of things will change especially the relationship between the grandmother and daughter because of the series of events that happened before Angela left town. She sat down on the dining chair, waiting for Ashley to fix her a cup of tea. "Mom, you can call her if you miss her that much," Ashley told her mother, grandma Peaches never admitted it with her mouth, but her actions spoke louder than words. .

"She didn't even call me when she arrived." Grandma Peaches admitted her pain.

"I'm her mother and she did not call me either, I only got the information from her father."

Grandma Peaches was not convinced.

"You can make Angela come back tomorrow if you want to." Ashley stifled a laugh.

"How?" Grandma Peaches asked.

"Give me the go-ahead and I will call her panicking that you were rushed to the hospital. Angela will get here with the next available train. Then you can be reunited with your granddaughter again."

Ashley burst into laughter.

"That will be a show to watch." Tina came in laughing. "The expression on Angela's face when she realizes it was a prank will be priceless. She cannot even get mad." She walked towards the dining table and placed a quick kiss on grandma Peaches cheeks, "Good morning grandma Peaches, good morning Aunt Ashley."

"Good Morning" they chorused.

"I have to go now, I have a meeting, a new media house wanted me to be influencing for them. If this clicks, it will be huge." She announced.

"You should at least look decent on your first meeting with them, what is this you are wearing?" she asked Tina. Tina was putting on sweatpants and a crop top, her stomach wasn't too revealing, she had makeup on and her braids packed in a bun.

"What is wrong with what I am putting on grandma Peaches?" she asked her grandmother. "It is a media house, not some nine to five companies or a church and besides it is a remote job." She explained. "Or what do you think I should wear, one of those maxi gowns you give to Angela?" she grabbed an apple from the table and laughed as she left the house. Ashley smiled to herself. She had always liked how Tina stood up for herself whether she was wrong or right. She was audacious and took responsibility for her actions boldly. Grandma Peaches phone rang. "My phone," she told Ashley "It is on the center table in the living room"

Ashley rushed down and brought the phone, "It's Angela." Grandma Peaches took the phone from Ashley quickly and answered the call.

"Grandma Peaches." She called.

"Yes, my baby" grandma Peaches replied.

"I'm sorry I haven't called you since I left, when I got here, I was so tired and fell asleep immediately, since then I have been sleeping all day while dad is at work."

"The Lord is your strength, my dear, Spencer shouldn't let you stay home alone all day." Grandma Peaches told her.

"Yeah, he has been seriously working on a presentation in his office; he said we will work something out by the weekend. I promise to take a stroll around the neighborhood today." She promised her grandmother.

"Hello! I'm here." Ashley shouted.

"Mom."

Grandma Peaches handed the phone to her daughter.

"How is your father?" Ashley asked.

"Missing you, he is buried in his work, maybe if you were here, you will help him relax. I know you will not let him work so hard, he doesn't even have time for himself." Angela replied to her mother. She was intentional with her words; she wanted her mother to have a reason to go back to her father.

"That's why you are there, your presence in his life will help him reduce his workaholic attitude," she told her daughter.

"There is only a little I can do, I'm his child, and you are his wife." Angela fired back. "It would have been nicer if you were here though, we would be together as a complete family."

"Angela, you have been there only a few days and you are already saying these things, what is he feeding you with?" she asked.

"Nothing. I have a mind of my mother; remember the bible passage that talked about how a virtuous woman builds her

home?" Angela asked. "Let's forget about that, how have you been?" she asked her mother. Ashley was silent. "I'm sorry I didn't call you when I arrived, I'm sure dad explained to you." She continued. "I will have opted for a video call but I do not like how my face looks right now, I want it to be that the next time you see me, I will be looking brighter."

"You are still crying?" Ashley asked.

"No mom" she lied. "I just want my face to look brighter."

"Ok baby, let me give the phone back to your grandma. If you didn't call when you did, mom will have fallen sick, you will have had to come back for emergency care." Ashley laughed.

"That's not true!" grandma Peaches defended herself.

"Please call her often." Ashley gave the phone back to grandma Peaches and continued what she was doing.

"It's not true, yes, I miss you but you wouldn't have been called back for emergency care because I can't fall sick, I am working in the supernatural."

"I believe you grandma" Angela laughed. Grandma Peaches barely fell sick.

"Is Tina around?" Angela asked.

"She left a while ago, just before you called. You both haven't talked?" Grandma Peaches asked Angela.

"No." she felt sad. "I haven't spoken to Michelle either, I will call them later."

"Ok grandma, I have to go now, I will talk to you later." "Bye!" Grandma Peaches said and Angela ended the call.

This is for the best grandma Peaches said to herself.

Angela stood up from the bed; she picked up her bible and placed it carefully on the bedside stool. Then preceded to making the bed, when she was done, she went into the kitchen to find something to eat. Her dad had dropped a piece of paper on the kitchen table.

I made scrambled eggs; it's in the microwave, Enjoy it with some bread and a cup of tea.

XoXo ~ Dad

She smiled to herself, her father didn't even bother to wake her up before he left for work, it gave her a feeling that he knew she barely slept at night and she had to use the morning hours to cover up for the lack of sleep she had every night. After eating, she went into her room and freshened up. Put on the same clothes and left the house, she had promised herself that she will leave the house in spite of her condition and explore the neighborhood; it will keep her from thinking and crying all day.

Angela had not even gone far, she was beginning to enjoy the environment and scenery when her phone rang. It was her dad.

"Good morning dad." She greeted him.

"Good morning baby girl, are you home?" he asked.

"No, I'm taking a walk in the neighborhood."

"Well, I'm sorry to cut your walk short but Richard is in the house, I asked him to help me get something from my study." "Is he your errand boy?" she asked. She noticed her father always brought him home, ask him to help do stuffs and they even went to the train station together to pick her up.

"Angela."

"I'm sorry daddy, I didn't mean to be rude, and the question was birthed out of pure curiosity." She stated. She wasn't lying.

"He is not my errand boy, he works with me. We are on the same team working together on a presentation, he is the only one I trust completely and that is why he has access to my home, now can you please go back home, he is waiting." "Ok." She turned immediately and began to walk home.

Richard was standing impatiently in the front of the house.

"Good morning." She greeted first. He didn't notice her approach.

"Good morning to you too." He answered.

She quickly brought out the keys and began to work her way into opening the door, maybe she became anxious because she knew he was in a hurry, the key fell from her hands.

"Let me help you with that." He bent down to pick up the keys and opened the door.

"Thanks." She appreciated him and they both entered the house. "I'm sure you know your way around, if you need anything, I will be in my room." She told him.

"Sure, thanks." After a few minutes, Richard called out to

Angela. "I'm done, come lock the door."

She came out almost immediately. "Ok. Bye."

Just before he left, he turned and said to her, "Your dad said you took a stroll, I guess you are trying to familiarize yourself around here."

"Yeah."

"Well if you don't mind, I can show you around on Saturday.

It's the least I could do."

"I do not want to be a bother." She waved it off.

"You didn't ask me, I offered to help." He persisted.

"Ok, Saturday it is then. See you." He left and she locked the door.

She went to her room to rest but the thoughts of everything began to flood through her mind. She thought of Charles and the moments they spent together, she imagined what their child would have looked like if it had lived. These were the thoughts that hunted her every single time she was alone, she couldn't help it by not thinking about them. She knew she couldn't continue that way so she stood up and started to sing songs of worship to God.

Oh the never overwhelming, never-ending

Reckless Love of God

Oh it chases me, fights till I'm found

Leaves the ninety-nine

I couldn't earn it, I don't deserve it

Still, you gave your life away

Oh the overwhelming, never-ending reckless love of God

She moved on from that song to another and another until she became completely lost in the spirit and began to speak in tongues. That evening when Spencer came back from work, they both sat down in the sitting room, bonding like they did every day.

"I think you should see a therapist, it will help you in your journey to healing. I am your father and I know that there are some things you will refrain from telling me. Besides, I cannot have you sitting home all day."

Angela was quiet, she was unsure.

"I want what is best for you dear."

"Dad, I don't know." She said.

"You will not know until you try it out. Maybe when you are much better than you are now, we could start hunting for a job for you."

"Ok."

"So, did you continue your walk today?"

"I didn't bother to, Richard promised to show me around on Saturday. I will wait, it's three days away."

"Richard huh?" Spencer tried to hide his smile but ended up with a smirk.

"Yeah Richard, anything wrong with that?" she asked her father, she understood what her father was insinuating but it was nothing of such. She wasn't even looking in the direction of a relationship with anyone not to think of Richard, the guy who takes walks with her father.

"No, nothing. Good night." He stood up and left her in the sitting room.

Angela picked up the remote and began to surf through the channels until she settled on a movie and began to watch it.

CHAPTER TWENTY

A NEW LIFE

Saturday came in a flash; Richard drove to Spencer's house to pick Angela up. They did not agree on a particular time and he did not have a number to contact her. Richard did not know how Spencer would react if he called to ask for her, and asked him to give her a message. When he got there, Spencer opened the door for him and informed him that Angela was still in her room and he will inform her about his presence.
"Thank you." Richard thanked Spencer.

"No, thank you. I really appreciate what you are doing."

Angela came out of her room singing, "Good morning, sorry for keeping you waiting." She apologized to Richard.

She was wearing a palazzo pant, a spaghetti hand top and a jean jacket to cover up her arms.

"It's not like we agreed on a particular time," he said in her defense

"You have a nice voice, you are in the choir?" he asked. "Was." She

stated.

She picked up her bag and kissed her father on his cheek. "Bye,

daddy."
"Bring her back safe," Spencer told Richard and they left.

The day was fun; Richard was such good company. They apologized

to each other again about their first encounter and decided to begin

their friendship on a new slate. They drove around, showed her

some landmarks, and told her the name of each street and some

recreational spots. They stopped by an ice cream spot and bought

some, they sat down and talked about their selves, Richard told her

about his family and the nature of his job with her father while Angela

talked about her family too especially about grandma Peaches and

Tina. When they were done, they decided to go back home.

"So which church are you attending tomorrow?" Richard asked

her. "I don't know yet, my dad use to attend Light Gate church,

I don't know if he has changed because he changed his house. I

think I will just get ready and go with him to wherever he goes."

She chuckled.

"Well, I hope I'm not pushing but let me invite you to my church tomorrow, you will love it." He smiled. "I will pick you up by seven." He offered.

"First of all, I don't know how dad will feel about it, but, what the name of your church is?" she asked.
"Ambassadors of Christ Youth Ministry." He answered.

"Youth church." She stated.

"Anything wrong with it?" He asked.

"I don't know. My grandma warned me to avoid those kind of churches when I was going to college then, she said in those kind of churches, they encourage youths to participate in sinful activities using grace as a cover-up." She gave a box smile while sharing her Grandma's warning to her. "Well, Angela, have you ever attended a youth church before?" He asked her.
"No." She answered him.

"Because grandma says so," he nods his head, "I think you shouldn't judge a book by its cover and you should attend one and judge for yourself." Angela was quiet.

"I will pick you up by seven?" He asked her.

"Yeah."

Richard pulled over in front of her house and they both got out of the car. He escorted her to the front door and also informed Spencer that he had brought his daughter home.

Angela went with Richard to church the next day and just like she had predicted, the topic was "*Grace.*" She raised her head to look at Richard and smiled, he raised his brows in return. "I guess God was aware of our conversation yesterday." He whispered. Angela promised herself to listen with an open heart, not to be judgmental and end up missing out on the blessings. When the service was over, she was glad she attended. She had never heard any preacher talk about grace according to what she heard before, it wasn't like she listened to lots of preachers anyways. Grandma Peaches would always say, "Protect your thoughts, it is not everyone you listen to, not everyone is called by God." She knew Grandma Peaches was only trying to protect her but since the turn of events, she saw reasons why Tina always argued with some of her beliefs. The first thing the pastor said was, "Grace is not an excuse for sin." She and Richard looked at each other. He went further by saying,

"God sent his only son to die for our sins, to bring us grace, that doesn't mean that we should go ahead and sin because

Jesus paid the price, but it simply means whenever we as Christians stumble and earnestly retrace our steps, the blood which had been shed on the cross of Calvary will atone for us."

By the time the pastor was done, the whole church was quiet. Angela also stood up as a first-timer and was welcomed warmly. After the service, someone came to her and briefly shared the word of God with her, took her contact and told her he hoped to see her in their weekly activities.

"Great church." She told Richard when they sat inside his car.

"Hopefully you will come again." He told her.

"I definitely will, it's not like I have another church I am attending here." She laughed.

Three Months Later

"Hey, guys!" Angela sat in front of her laptop. Michelle and Tina had been hanging out together, Tina had gone to visit Michelle in her house and they decided to place a call through to Angela.

"Look who is looking fresher and fresher by the day," Tina said to Angela.
"That is no excuse to steal my best friend," Angela told her.

"She is jealous." Michelle laughed. "How is it going over there?" she asked.

"Truthfully, I never knew I would like it this much. Therapy is going great, I'm happy in my new church, finally got to join the choir again and meeting new people." "Hmm." Tina nodded her head.
"That's great," Michelle added. "Tell us about this new guy."

"Which new guy?" Angela asked in confusion, she wasn't seeing anyone.

"The one you have been hanging out with, hello." Tina widened her eyes.
"Richard?" she asked.

"You tell us," Michelle reacted.

"Richard is just a friend. I do not like him that way."

"We always consider the good guys as just friends and fall for the bad ones." Tina rolled her eyes.
"Tina" Michelle scolded.

"What? That was the situation between her and Isaiah." Tina replied to them. "I know it stroke a chord, but it is the truth."

"It's just been three months," Angela answered her. "I know I cannot dictate for you how to handle pain, especially the ones that have to do with our emotions but you have to look to the future the past is in the past." Tina frankly said to her. "She is right Angela. Besides, according to you, Richard is a church boy and he is family-oriented too, he works with your dad which means he has a decent job. Isn't that what you have always wanted?" Michelle chipped in.

"Or is there something about him that is off?" Tina asked.

"No, not at all," Angela answered. "We are just friends, he hasn't said anything to me yet and that is why I never really thought about it. Above all, I want to work according to God's plan. I no longer want to take charge of my life, I gave him the wheel." Angela told them. She did not want to be pressured into anything. "Besides I do not know what he will think of me when he finds out about my past." "You will tell him," Tina replied.

"You should also pray about it," Michelle told her.

"Well, there is a big announcement." Tina's face lit up.

"Tell me about it." Angela smiled.

"You are going to be a godmother soon," Michelle announced.

"Whoa! Congratulations!"

The three ladies continued to converse and talked about moments they have missed in each other's life

After the video chat, Angela continued to draft some application letters for some openings she saw online. She was ready to get back to work. Her phone rang and she picked it up.

"Hey Richard, good afternoon." She greeted him.

"I'm outside, kindly open the door ma'am." He said to Angela.

"Ok, did my father ask you to get something?" She asked on the phone as she stood to get the door open.

"No, I came to see you." He gave a quick response, while she opened the door.

"Feel free to enter." She offered and he did happily.

Angela noticed the unsettled look on Richard's face, she wanted to know what he came to see her for. "You said you've come to see me." She prompted him to speak.

"Can't I come to see you?" he asked her.

"Of course, you can but this is your work hours, so it must be important and that is why I'm curious." She told him.

"I love you." He said quietly.

"Hmm?" She looked at him, pretending as if she did not hear what he said. "Look, these feelings are not very new and I have absolutely no idea what to do about them." He held her hands.

"I have prayed about it and I have told God to take them away if it is not in his plan but every time I see you, they continue to intensify." "I do not know what to say." She told him.

"You do not have to say anything, for now, you can sit back and pray about it. You know I am not the kind of person who wanted to date around, I want to build a family, a nation that will be an army for Christ and I cannot do that with just anyone but with someone who loves God as much as I do and understands the kind of person I am."

"There is so much you do not know about me." She told him. "Then tell me." He urged her. Angela told Richard about her whole past, everything that had happened. When she was done, Richard told her, "Everyone has a past, it doesn't define your present and future.

The woman sitting in front of me loves God, and she loves him genuinely but if you want, we could both sit back and pray about it."

"I agree with that, I think I need to speak to my Fathers about It." She calmly said to him.
"Fathers?" he asked her.

"Yeah, heavenly and earthly." They both laughed. "I love you, Angela." He told her.

Angela does not look surprised to hear that anymore, and to Richard's surprise he heard Angela say to him, "I think I am in love with you too." The two kept on looking at each other, and after some seconds, Angela shies away, while they both laughed.